# THE SPY AND HIS LADY LOVE

## A SEABROOK FAMILY SAGA, BOOK SEVEN

## CHRISTINE DONOVAN

Dear Readers,

Thank you for purchasing THE SPY AND HIS LADY LOVE. I apologize for any historical inaccuracies as they are made solely by the author to better suit the story.

I hope you enjoy reading it as much as I did writing it.

This book is dedicated to all my readers. You give me the inspiration to write. Thank you from the bottom of my heart!

❧ Created with Vellum

# SUMMARY

Penelope Hemlock, the natural-born daughter of the deceased 4th Duke of Wentworth, finds herself welcome within the new duke's family, once they know of her existence. The 5th Duke, Thomas Seabrook, insists she has a season and dares anyone to question the title of Lady before her name. In no time, she's dining and dancing in the aristocracy's company, especially one mysterious and damaged duke.

Harry Sinclair, the Duke of Newbury, fought alongside Wellington at Waterloo. As he convalesces from his battle injuries, he finds himself thrown into the life of a peer. He never expected to inherit his uncle's title, nor did he want it. Bored with the leisurely life of a duke, Harry continues serving King and Crown in a new position as a spy. Who would ever suspect a scarred, one eyed, lame legged duke to be a spy? Nor would one believe he was duchess hunting. Since he now held the title of duke, he needed an heir and a spare.

Even with his supposed flaws, Wentworth set his sights on Harry for his illegitimate sister. Harry and his cousin, Hugh Sinclair, both pay homage to Penelope. When Penelope uncovers the truth of Harry and Hugh's identity and deceit, can she forgive and allow love to enter her heart? Or will bitterness and hatred tear her heart apart, never to be whole again?

# CHAPTER 1

"Who is the man dancing with Lady Elizabeth Spencer?" Penelope Hemlock asked her brother, Thomas Seabrook, the Duke of Wentworth.

"I've never set eyes on the gentleman before," Wentworth answered with curiosity steeped in his voice. "Isn't that the point of a masquerade ball? To be unrecognizable."

"He's holding Lady Elizabeth rather close and intimately as though he's quite familiar with her. She's the sister of one of your close friends. Do something, Thomas, before he causes a scandal."

Her brother's eyes pierced hers. "Pray tell, how do you know about intimacy and scandal since you were raised in the country and are only ten and seven?" Shaking his head, he said, "Never mind. I don't want to know."

Thankfully, the waltz had ended. "Excuse me, I'm going to follow them," Penelope murmured.

"Follow them..."

Penelope didn't hear the end of her brother's words as her curiosity, which had gotten her into trouble in the past, got the best of her. Following Elizabeth and the stranger took her out of the ballroom and into the dark shadowy hallways. Squinting into the ebony darkness from her hiding spot behind a potted palm, her face peeking out between the palm leaves, she saw silhouettes of figures while hushed whispers swirled throughout the air. Her eyes and ears strained to no avail. Too dark to recognize anyone, not that she really would, having only been in London a short time. Nor could she hear what secrets were being uttered.

Had that man taken Elizabeth into the shadows to compromise her? As her heart sped up and she prepared to enter the intimidating darkness to seek Elizabeth, a hand grabbed her upper arm roughly. She was spun around until she crashed into an unyielding wall of hard maleness.

"What do you think you are doing? Do you want some reprobate to think you're a doxy and take advantage of you?" The deep, intimidating voice sent shivers up and down her spine in both panic and awareness.

"I…I…beg your pardon." She shrugged her shoulder out of his reach. "I'm looking for someone. Not that it's any of your business."

He lowered his head. The man towered over her, and right before he breathed into her ear, she caught his sneer. "I believe your brother, the duke, would disagree. Shall we find him?"

Who was this man, and why was he making her his business? "No. I believe I will retreat back into the ballroom. Excuse me."

"Please, let me escort you. I believe I hear a waltz playing, and I would enjoy your company on the dance floor."

Before Penelope could protest and refuse the dance, he was leading her into the dimly lit ballroom amongst a crush of bodies. She prayed her recent dance lessons were fortuitous as this was the first time she'd danced a waltz with someone other than her dancing master. She also hoped no one recognized her as it was forbidden to dance a waltz before receiving permission from one of the patronesses of Almacks. And she wasn't attending Almacks until Wednesday next. Of course she never imagined being accepted into Almacks. But as usual Wentworth's name and money opened doors.

"Relax, I will not ravish you." The deep timbre of his voice did strange things to her insides.

"It's not that. I'm embarrassed to admit this is my first waltz." Too bad a mask covered most of his face. A face she believed would be handsome.

"You are dancing splendidly. The duke got his money's worth."

Penelope frowned. "You have me at a disadvantage. You appear to know who I am, but I don't know you. Pray, tell me your name?" She waited with bated breath for his answer. And waited and waited.

When she'd nearly given up, he replied, "You may call me Hugh."

"Hugh...?" Most men flaunted their family name, making her wonder why all the secrecy.

He chuckled. "Your inquisitive nature will get you in trouble. I'm surprised Wentworth has not lectured you about it."

Heat crept up her cheeks. Not that he could see with her mask coving the top half of her face. "I've done my best to hide that part of my personality from him."

"Well done, my dear. But I expect you won't be able to for long."

The more she listened to Hugh speak, the more he sounded familiar, even though she couldn't have possibly met him before. His name rang no bells or warnings inside her head. Although she had to ask, "Have we met before?"

He cocked his head and studied her eyes as he led her into a twirl. "No. But I'm aware of your family. Wentworth is a powerful and respected duke. And you have only recently come under his protection."

An inferno encompassed her entire body. No doubt this man knew her shame. "'Bastard'. You may say it. It will not be the first or last time someone refers to me as it. I realize I am tarnished goods and will be near impossible to marry off, even with my sizable dowry." Her stomach tightened and her chest began to ache as she waited for this stranger's response.

Wentworth believed adopting her into the home of her dead father and renaming her, Lady Penelope Seabrook, would open all avenues for her. Would make up for their father's indiscretion and the station of her birth. That an overly large dowry would make men ignore what she was. She went along with him. He'd given her no choice. That didn't make her believe him.

"Forgive me, Lady Penelope if I gave you the impression of disrespect. I meant no such thing by referring to your family and how you came about to be a part of it. Also, you should know, I do not judge people by the circumstances of their birth. Some of the highest born people of the aristocracy are not worth my time." As the music ended, he asked, "May I escort you back to your brother?"

"That would be lovely."

Wentworth looked in deep conversation with his duchess, so her dance partner bowed off and made haste, she noticed, in the general direction of the darkness. Had he attended tonight's masquerade with his mistress? Had she been awaiting his attentions in the shadows while they danced? She refused to acknowledge the slight panic in her heart. She had no interest in the man. Or did she?

"Did you enjoy yourself this evening, Penelope?" Emma, the Duchess of Wentworth, queried during the carriage ride home.

"Yes. Although I didn't see the point of my being here this evening as I couldn't tell who anyone was."

Wentworth, who sat opposite her and beside his wife, said, "Precisely. I wanted your first venture into society to be under the cover of a mask. I wanted you to be at ease. I didn't want all occupants of the room to stop speaking and stare at you when you entered. Which, I might add, will happen. People will go out of their way to snub you and make you feel inferior. Tonight I wanted you to have fun and dance."

"Thank you, I think." She'd been warned about members of the ton and how they would treat her with disdain and cut her direct. She'd yet to witness it. Since Wentworth had rescued her from poverty after her mother passed, she'd attended only intimate dinners held in their home. Or a home of a family friend. Tonight was her first foray into public, and she'd survived intact. Next time she best prepare to be crucified.

Relieved that no one recognized his true identity, Harry Sinclair, left Lady Penelope with her preoccupied brother. No one knew that the Duke of Newbury, Harry Sinclair, didn't really have a cousin named Hugh. The disguise was a convenient way to do undercover work for the War Office and for Harry to go about town without having to pretend to be the crippled duke. The man all of the *ton* pitied and stayed away from.

After he left Penelope he continued watching her from the outer fringes where dimly lit ballroom met darkness. He didn't want to admit how much she intrigued him with her innocence, quick wit, and inquisitive nature. If only he could protect her from members of the aristocracy when Wentworth introduced her out in polite society for the first time. Tonight didn't count as it involved masks.

He had hoped Mr. Smythe would be in attendance because he had secret business to discuss with the head of the Bow Street Runners—business he didn't want anyone to know about. This would've been the perfect place to conduct such a clandestine meeting. Mr. Smythe had had the good fortune of marrying the granddaughter of a countess and being welcomed into the inner circle of Wentworth's friends.

Perhaps tomorrow night would bring on the opportunity. Wentworth planned another small gathering at his estate for the evening meal. Another gathering, Harry believed, to find a worthy husband for Penelope. The duke had an excellent head on his shoulders. The sooner he married off the natural-born daughter of the late duke, the better. Harry would hate to see Penelope hurt by the beau monde. He was in the market for a wife. Perhaps he would consider her. After all, she was quite comely.

When the hired hack dropped him off down the block from his home on Park Street, Harry paid the driver, pulled the collar up on his black cloak, and lowered the brim of his hat at the same time he removed the mask. His eyes and ears on high alert, he scanned the street and surrounding homes, looking and listening for anything out of the ordinary. Having two identities, and oftentimes more, made Harry diligent when guarding his secret life. If not, he could find himself dead and his body dumped in the Thames. Icy chills snaked up his spine causing him to shiver. He was mortal, after all, and not above being murdered. He'd had a pleasant life until now, and he intended to keep living it on his own terms.

Having convinced himself no danger lurked in the darkness, he snuck through private yards and gardens, through openings in fences and onto his property. He entered his estate through a hidden door into a secret hallway that led into his private chambers.

"Welcome home, Your Grace," cried Harry's valet, Edmond, in relief. Edmond may be his valet, but his proper occupation was working for the War Office as a spy under his command. He and Harry served in the army under Wellington and fought alongside each other at Waterloo.

"Thank you, Edmond. You may retire for the night. I'm staying in and no longer need your services this evening."

Edmond bowed. "Goodnight, Your Grace."

There were times Harry still forgot he'd inherited his uncle's dukedom. His grandparents must be rolling over in their graves at the turn of events. Their second son and the black sheep of the family had run off and married a peasant's daughter. Conceived one child, a son, and that son was now the feared and pitied Duke of Newbury. Only several people knew the accurate story. Harry intended keeping it that way.

# CHAPTER 2

"WELCOME, YOUR GRACE, TO WENTWORTH MANOR." HARRY hid his surprise at being greeted in the great hall by none other than his hostess, the American Duchess.

He bowed as best he could with his leg braced up, not allowing him to bend at the knee. "Your Grace." She genuinely smiled at him with a warm welcome, and his esteem of her climbed quite high. "Thank you for inviting me into your home."

"You're very welcome. May I impose upon you to escort me into the drawing room? It appears I'm rather tardy to the festivities."

"My pleasure, I assure you." Harry held out his arm, and the duchess didn't hesitate to place her gloved hand on his forearm. "Before we go, may I inquire of you to allow my valet, Edmond, to join your servants in their evening meal?"

"Not at all." She addressed Edmond directly. "Down the hall. Go through the kitchen and you will find them." She turned her beautiful smile on Harry, and he found himself envious of her husband. "Shall we?"

They ascended the staircase. Her slow and graceful and

he slow and awkward. If the lame leg wasn't bad enough, only seeing out of one eye because of his black patch made it even worse. Not to mention the itch from the theater makeup he used to create his hideous scar—something he'd become adept at. She led him into a large burgundy drawing room noisily full of people.

"Here we are." Her Grace removed her arm from his and curtsied. "I will send my husband along."

He watched her weave in and around several occupants until she reached Wentworth's side. Heads close together as they shared private words, Wentworth glanced his way, bowed to his wife, and strolled towards Harry, pausing briefly to speak to one guest or another. Harry recognized most occupants of the room, even if he hadn't been formally introduced to them. He knew they invited him for only one reason. Wentworth wanted a match between him and Lady Penelope. Although if that were so, why, pray tell, was Viscount Dayton and Mr. Phillip Percy in attendance? Here was the man to ask.

"Newbury." Wentworth nodded his head in greeting. "I'm glad you could make it this evening. And a lovely evening it is."

Nodding his head in return, Harry replied, "Thank you for inviting me. It's a lovely evening, but my leg tells me it will rain by midnight." Harry did not know if it would rain by midnight, but it was London and it almost always rained. He had to play the cripple and all that went with it. Such as predicting the rain due to arthritic pain.

"I imagine you are right on that account. I believe my sister, Lady Penelope, will be thrilled to renew your acquaintance this evening. Now if you'll excuse me." Wentworth tipped his head forward. "Duty calls."

As a servant walked by with a round tray covered in champagne flutes, Harry plucked one off the tray and took a large sip, ignoring the bubbles tickling his nose as he scanned the crowd. He was not surprised to see Wentworth's sister, Lady Northborough, and her husband, Lord Northborough, as strangers called him. But to his friends, Myles. Harry wondered where he would fall once they became acquainted? Friends, he hoped. From what he knew about Myles and his reputation, Harry believed they would indeed become excellent friends. The scandal sheets had not exaggerated his wife, Isabella's beauty. She could make a man kill himself for want of her. Or so he'd heard.

With the couple stood young Penelope looking lovely and innocent dressed in white. Although once at the mercy of the lecher, Viscount Hadley, Harry wondered how innocent. He'd done his homework. With his spy credentials, nothing or no one was beyond his reach. Viscount Hadley used and abused his servants, both sexually and physically. The man deserved to rot in Newgate. Perhaps Penelope, with his help, would be the one to put him there. He only hoped the viscount hadn't abused Penelope. No one deserved such a fate.

Her soft, animated voice traveled through the air and warmed him. It didn't matter if he couldn't make out what she said, hearing the tone proved enough to entertain him. As far as Harry could tell, the only downfall to this evening was his attire—dressed as the injured, lame, and hideous Duke of Newbury. How could he possibly win over Penelope? He never would consider taking a wife if he hadn't inherited the dukedom and all the responsibility that went with it—an heir and a spare. Prinny hinted at wives and heirs and spares every time they spoke. The Prince Regent knew his secret, so it was easy for him to believe Harry could attract a wife.

Bored and standing on the fringes of society, in more ways than one, Harry hobbled over to Wentworth who had joined Penelope. The banging of his cane connecting with the wooden floor had all eyes turned his way causing him to cringe. Oh, how he hated the pitying looks on their faces.

"Wentworth, may I beg a formal introduction to your guests?"

"How remiss me ." Wentworth said. "Your Grace, may I present Lord and Lady Northborough," then he turned to face his sister and brother-in-law "Isabella, Myles, the Duke of Newbury."

"Countess." Harry rigidly bowed. "It is a pleasure to make your acquaintance."

"And I yours, Your Grace," Lady Northborough replied with a smile that didn't quite reach her eyes. Harry didn't blame her. She must wonder how her brother could hope for a match between him and Penelope. Many others must wonder the same thing. What did Wentworth know others didn't? Was there a chance he knew his true identity? Impossible. Not unless Wentworth had a secret identity as well. If he did, Surely Harry would know.

He inclined his head to Northborough. "A pleasure to meet you, Northborough."

Northborough nodded his head. "Yes." The earl's eyes looked him over from head to toe. "Did you sustain your injuries fighting Bonaparte at Waterloo?"

Harry hid a chuckle when Northborough's wife elbowed him in the side then looked at Harry, blushing a becoming shade of pink. Wentworth cleared his throat and said, "Excuse Myles. He has a habit of speaking before he thinks."

"Quite all right," Harry said with a grin. "I'd rather people acknowledge my disfigurement openly than pretend I'm fit as a fiddle. And the answer to your question is, yes. I sustained my injuries at Waterloo. A particularly nasty battle."

"The gash on your face looks rather recent," Penelope said, which brought gasps to everyone's mouths.

"It is, and it isn't. I reopened the old scar recently after taking a rather nasty fall. Having one eye and a leg which refuses to bend makes me clumsy." He chuckled, which he turned into a coughing fit. Must not have them thinking he was healthy inside. Unhealthy inside and out and a rich duke. Excellent marriage material. If Wentworth believed it numbered his days, he was more likely to convince his sister to marry him. Convince her he would not live long. She would be a young, rich widow and then could marry for love. Love…what a silly notion that some members of the ton held out for love. Harry only needed a willing wife to give him an heir and spare. He got everything else he needed from his childhood friend and mistress, Rose. Thinking of Rose, when and if he married, would he break his marriage vows by keeping a mistress? He didn't believe so.

Why had he decided to pursue Penelope? Because he had no other prospects and she intrigued him because of her background. She appeared to have a bright spark inside. And he couldn't forget beauty. If he was inclined to lose his head or heart to a woman, it could be Penelope. Good thing he wasn't so inclined. Another reason she suited his purpose was he didn't want a spoiled young lady of privilege who hadn't a mind of her own. One who expected her suitor to spoil her and treat her like a princess. No indeed. Penelope would not expect that of a prospective husband.

"Does it hurt?" Penelope's velvety voice intruded on his musings.

This time Wentworth interceded on his behalf. "Newbury is not here to answer questions about his injuries. Perhaps there are other, more appropriate questions you'd prefer to ask him?" But further questioning of any kind was stalled by the announcement dinner was served.

Harry escorted the Duchess of Wentworth into the large, stately dining room and was pleased to be seated beside her with Penelope on his other side. Sitting across from someone was nice as you could enjoy the view, but conversations across dinner tables were forbidden. Now he could engage Penelope in light conversation and get to know her better. He had thought about her constantly since dancing with her at the masquerade. Not that she would know Hugh who she met the other night, and he, were one and the same. Something that would only be disclosed if they did become betrothed.

COULD the night get any worse? Penelope mused to herself as she found herself sitting beside the hideous duke at the spacious dining table. Well, that was rather harsh. He was only hideous on one side of his face. The side facing her. The other side was handsome. How unfortunate to be disfigured. His thick, dark hair hung loose to his chin, no doubt to help in hiding his black patch and scar. Fortunately for him, when sitting down one didn't notice his lame leg. Perhaps if she sat on his good side she could forget, for a time, about his shortcomings.

Sitting next to him now, she wondered if he was a good conservationist. "Your Grace," Penelope said as the first course landed in front of them. "What have you been doing the past several years to occupy your time since leaving the army?"

Pausing midway to his mouth with a spoon full of turtle soup, he hesitated then continued on with his soup. It took several moments before he placed his spoon down next to his bowl, removed his napkin from his lap, and dabbed at the corners of his mouth with large, powerful hands. For a man with such robust hands, his movement was surprisingly graceful. She could almost forget about his shortcomings.

He didn't bother to turn toward her. His lips did, however, turn up into a smirk or smile, she couldn't tell which. "I keep busy. Between my many holdings and being a duke and all that entails, the socializing, the House of Lords and such, I find I have little time to myself. Which is good."

"Why is not having time to yourself good, Your Grace?"

"What an inquisitive mind you have, Lady Penelope."

Something about the way he said it made her wonder where she had heard someone say those same words to her before. It would come to her in time. His mannerisms were familiar as well, and she'd only dined with him one other time. She wasn't proud of herself for how she'd acted that night at Spencer House. Penelope knew they attended only so Wentworth could meet the allusive duke and gauge whether he would be marriage material for her. It seemed the duke passed her brother's test because here he was seated next to her. She would try to keep an open mind about the duke. She, who really had no right to be considering taking a duke for a husband, her being a bastard and all.

Unfortunately, being born a bastard did not take away one's pride. And Penelope had pride enough for two. Not to mention stubbornness and her curious nature. She may understand her station in life, even if her family ignored it. Just because they had accepted her, didn't mean other members of the ton would.

"I should apologize for my curiosity, but it won't do any good."

Now he turned his head. His one starling blue eye unsettled her. Along with his smile. A genuine smile that had her tingling because truly his handsomeness and how it affected her shocked her. She couldn't possibly be attracted to this man. The disfigured and pitied duke? She did admire him so.

Because if their lives were reversed, and she had his afflictions, she'd never leave the house. She would die an old spinster relying on the kindness of Wentworth.

"I beg your forgiveness for asking such a personal question. Perhaps we should eat before the food gets cold," she mumbled.

"Yes, indeed. Perhaps we should." Was that amusement she heard in his voice?

For what seemed like an eternity, one course after the next came and went and Penelope barely nibbled on the food. She was ashamed of herself for thinking unkind things about the duke after glimpsing the kind gentleman behind his shortcomings. She didn't mean shortcomings as insulting, she couldn't come up with a sufficient word to use. He deserved everyone's respect for the war hero he was. And she felt so beneath him. How could Wentworth think the duke would consider marrying her? A bastard nobody who was far from innocent by ton standards.

It took forever for the ladies to leave the gentlemen to their cheroots and brandy and retire to the drawing room for gossip. Emma and Penelope sat together on a mauve velvet settee. Penelope glanced across the room to the two young ladies who'd joined them. One could not have an uneven number of males and females for dinner. Wentworth had invited eligible ladies also looking for husbands. Viscount Dayton and Mr. Percy were in the market for wives.

"Do you think Lady Julia Finley and Miss Sophia Trembley were horrified when the Duke of Newbury arrived?" Penelope queried.

"I'm quite convinced they were," Emma replied, "but both ladies hid their feelings well. Even with his...issues...His Grace is still quite a catch. If you concentrate on his good side, he is strikingly handsome."

"Emma?"

"Not as handsome as my duke, but handsome, none-theless if you don't look too closely at his scar and eye patch and forgot his injured leg. Some people compare him to a pirate. What young lady doesn't dream of a handsome, dangerous, debonair pirate kidnapping her and sailing off into the sunset to a deserted island so he can claim her as his?"

She couldn't hide her giggles. "No wonder you write and sell so many gothic novels."

"Shhh. Please remember it's under a false name and not everyone in the family knows. However, talking about pirates has let lose my imagination. I can hardly wait to retire and put pen to ink. My faithful readers will love a good trea-sure hunt with a handsome pirate. I will make him a good pirate who works for the Crown. The Crown sends him on the hunt for the notorious Blackbeard. While sailing through a storm he rescues a fair maiden from a sinking vessel bound for the Americas. Little does the good pirate, I shall call him Scarborough, realize the fair maiden is actually Blackbeard's eldest daughter."

Penelope sighed and her body turned languid. "When can I read it?"

Emma laughed. "I have not written a word. But thank you for helping me come up with a plot. Here are the gentlemen returning to us. Really, if you look closely at the Duke of Newbury and past his afflictions, he is handsome like my pirate will be. I think I'll model him after the duke."

If she looked closely enough, Penelope could see Newbury as a pirate. Although there was another man who reminded her of a pirate. Hugh, whom she'd danced with at the masquerade. With his mask and his devil-may-care atti-tude, he could very well be a real-day pirate.

"Pardon, Lady Penelope, Your Grace, I don't mean to

intrude," the Duke of Newbury said as he acknowledged both of them. "I was hoping to interest Lady Penelope in a game of chess?"

She could lie and say she didn't play when truth be told she loved chess. Had been taught when in Viscount Hadley's employ by the old butler who had taken pity on her. They would play at night, and Penelope knew it was his way of looking out for her when her mother couldn't. "I would love to, Your Grace."

"Shall we, then?" Newbury said as he offered his hand, obviously the one not clutched to his cane. Never would she understand why ladies of the ton needed to act helpless when gentlemen were around. She was perfectly capable of standing up from a settee by herself. In fact, she did it many times a day. Such silly etiquette games society played. "Thank you." When their hands connected, an odd warm vibration traveled from beneath her glove, up her arm, and settled inside her chest. How odd. Hands still joined, Penelope looked at him and he at her. A puzzled expression crossed his features momentarily. No doubt similar to the look she gave him. Pulling her hand back, she led the way to the chess table across the room, near a large picture window overlooking the back gardens. Although it was dark outside, Penelope knew the gardens were there as she'd taken refuge inside the terraced walls many times since arriving in London.

"White or black, my dear?"

Had he called her dear? She'd never been asked by a man what color she wanted before. They took it upon themselves to assume she wanted white. Or they wanted black. Either way, it was a novelty to be asked. When she played with one of her sisters, she took black. "Black."

His one eye glimmered with amusement. "Black for the lady it is."

"You don't mind?" She wished the words back the moment she spoke them.

"No. Why should I care? Black, white, it doesn't matter."

"It's my experience most men prefer black. They think white is the weaker color."

"Nonsense." He leaned slightly forward and whispered, "Don't you mean weaker sex by referring to the color white as being female?"

Her cheeks warmed. "Actually, I believe the weaker sex to be males." She lowered her eyes, afraid of what she might see.

Laughter, deep and throaty, rang out in the air. Her eyes popped up and her soft nervous giggles joined his laughter. "I don't believe anyone has ever found humor when I've expressed my thoughts about what sex is weaker."

"Pity, Lady Penelope. They obviously had no sense of fun or adventure."

"And you do, Your Grace?" Oh dear. She was flirting. But how could she not. His musical laughter did strange things to her insides.

His expression changed from amusement to seriousness in the blink of an eye. "One cannot live as I do without it. Shall we play?"

"Yes, of course." Penelope considered herself a better-than-average chess player. She'd often beat Wentworth or her other brother, Sebastian, who was presently visiting Scotland with his wife and the Dowager Duchess of Wentworth. Newbury put her skills to test. Five moves into the game he said, "Check Mate."

"Would you care for another game?" If someone had told her earlier today, she would enjoy the Duke of Newbury's company she would have told them they were daft.

"Thank you. Another time, perhaps." Leaning heavily on his cane, he awkwardly stood and bowed formally. "It was a pleasure. Goodnight, Lady Penelope." He paused and frowned thoughtfully. "I forgot to mention that you met my cousin, Mr. Hugh Sinclair, last night at the masquerade. He seems quite taken with you."

She hurried to stand and curtsy. "Goodnight, Your Grace."

Watching him leave, leaning heavily on his cane, but still appearing young, fit, and vibrant, Penelope puzzled. She couldn't believe the insufferable and intriguing gentleman she'd danced with last evening was related to Newbury. Or perhaps not. They seemed of the same build and height.

Once in bed, beneath the counterpane, her eyes closed, she envisioned Emma's pirate and he resembled Newbury right down to the scar. She found the pirate rather attractively handsome. And fell asleep having pleasant dreams of her and her pirate.

# CHAPTER 3

"How was your evening, Your Grace?" Edmond asked as they climbed into the carriage with the Newbury ducal crest painted on the sides.

"Surprisingly amusing."

His valet cocked a brow. "I would've thought the young ladies present would beg a headache to get out of dining with you."

Harry chuckled. "Actually no. Perhaps the other two young ladies in attendance would have if I'd sat next to them or lavished my attentions on them. However, I didn't pay them any heed. Now, Lady Penelope, she was like a breath of fresh air. She even proved a worthy chess opponent."

"Truly?"

"My surprise as well. Perhaps there is more to the young lady than I originally believed. Actually, between the other night and this evening, I do know there is more to her. She has none of the false silliness as other young debutants. Nor does she cringe away from hideous me. Neither does she seem jaded because of the circumstances from her birth. She doesn't hide the fact she's a bastard at all."

"Perhaps you have found your duchess?"

Days ago he didn't believe so. Today Harry hoped he had. Penelope stirred feelings inside him he'd thought dead and gone. Ever since leaving the army, he'd been numb inside. And when he wasn't numb, he had nightmares that could drive any sane man mad. Thank God he wasn't any man. And much of his return to sanity he owed to reading scientific textbooks and having studied and learned meditation. Also, his former mistress, Rose helped him. She'd known him since his childhood. Anyhow, some numbness was good. It made him an excellent spy. His feelings didn't get involved in his cases. He preferred it that way.

If he took Penelope for a wife, would he allow his budding feelings for her to surface? Could he deal with the onslaught of emotions? Hide his nightmares from her? Time would tell. Meanwhile, he'd send a missive to Wentworth asking for an audience. Time for marriage negotiations before some other bloke saw all Penelope had to offer. Regardless of her birth status, she came from a wealthy, influential, titled family. He needed to sign the betrothal papers before some poor aristocratic gentleman offered for her, spent her dowry, and shipped her off to the countryside to wallow and die. The sudden ache in his chest worried him.

SITTING at his large mahogany desk in his study, Harry's hand cradled a glass of fine scotch whiskey. He'd long since given up on getting any sleep tonight as his mind wouldn't settle down. Several things worried him. One being the case he was working on. The case of a highly regarded Baron rumored to have worked with Napoleon during the later years of the war. News had him still spying on his own country for the French even now.

The prince was beside himself as the Baron had spent many years at court as his confident. Now to hear rumors of his deceit and treason? The Regent wanted to see the Baron hang. Harry wanted to see the man hang for all the soldiers and innocent people who died because of his treasonous crimes. For his own injuries and those of his battalions as they fought valiantly at Waterloo.

Catching the Baron was why he wanted the Runner Smythe's help. Since Smythe had newly married into the Bridgeton family, he now had the opportunity to socialize with the aristocracy. Become acquainted with the Baron in a social setting. Not just at functions, but at clubs such as White's and Brooks's. It was rumored the Baron had a gambling problem, which could be the reason he sold English secrets. Not that Harry cared for the reason. Treason was treason any way one looked at it.

Harry couldn't go undercover himself. Baron Littleton would recognize him. And he would never believe Harry would go against the Crown. A Runner, one jaded and angry at being demoted, would be perfect. Hence, Smythe.

HARRY FOUND himself being escorted into Smythe's office on Bow Street in the Covent Garden Neighborhood. Not a big office for one so important and powerful.

"Your Grace." Smythe bowed and gestured toward a hard wooden chair facing his desk. "Please have a seat and tell me how I may help you today?"

Harry had thought long and hard about approaching Smythe as Hugh Sinclair, but if they were to work together, which he hoped they would, there couldn't be secrets between them. Even if it put him in a precarious situation, seeing's how he was friends with the Seabrooks. "I have come for an employment opportunity."

Clearly, he'd shocked the Runner as he sat down at his desk and looked puzzled. "I don't understand?" He paused and offered refreshments, for which Harry declined.

"May I be blunt?" Harry said, well…bluntly.

The Runner leaned forward, looking more curious than shocked now. "Yes. Please do."

"There are rumors I've worked for the War Office since the war ended with France."

"Yes. I heard as such."

"They are true. And I was hoping, with the head of the War Office's permission, to offer employment to you."

Smythe's jaw dropped. "Pardon, Your Grace, but did you offer me a job? You do realize I have one already."

Harry's chuckled. "Yes. However, I plan to have you demoted so you will quit and go undercover with me and my men to catch a spy. A spy for France who is at the top of our most treasonous list."

"Have me demoted? Want me to quit?" Smythe's eyes widened. "Forgive me if I seem shocked." He leaned forward. "The truth is, I am shocked."

"Rightly so. If I were in your shoes, I'd be shocked as well. Your name has come up several times at the War Office. You have been in our sights for potential employment for some time now. We," he cleared his throat, "*I* believe you would be an exceptional asset to our operation."

"What if I refuse? Will there be repercussions to my job here?" Smythe asked, looking uncomfortable.

"No. No demotion, no nothing. If you accept the job, the demotion I speak about would give you a cover story for wanting to commit treason against the Crown. If you decline the offer, nothing changes for you. However, please take some time to think it over. Although the work is dangerous, as your work is now, you would have more free time. I believe you are newly married, and I imagine the long hours of a Runner leave little time for your wife. Working for me is sporadic. The hours are unset and many times work happens out at social events in the evening."

Harry leaned on his cane to stand. He could not reveal himself until Smythe agreed to work with him. "Send word to me tomorrow, or better still." He placed his calling card on the Runner's desk. "Call upon my residence. Good day."

Once in his black carriage, Harry pondered what the Runner's answer would be. One moment he looked intrigued and the next shocked and uneasy. His answer was anybody's guess. Now off to the Duke of Wentworth's for his offer of marriage to Penelope.

THOMAS SEABROOK SAT in his study going over the account books his steward left with him after their morning meeting. The duke was pleased to see revenues from several of his holdings increasing and his tenants profiting nicely as well. The tenant farmers had suffered for years under his father's leadership. Thomas had been trying to make up for his father's mistakes since taking over the dukedom. Seeing progress pleased him. Lessoned the guilt he'd carried around for years since learning of his father's behavior, which nearly bankrupted them. If he'd not married his lovely American wife, Emma Hamilton, he might have found himself in debtors' prison. Not something he relished experiencing. How fortunate for him Emma fell in love with him and agreed to be his duchess even if the events following their nuptials had her threatening to sail back to Massachusetts and abandon him.

A knock on his study door snapped his mind back into focus. "Yes."

His butler opened the door, bowed, then handed him a card. "The Duke of Newbury to see you, Your Grace."

Thomas had been expecting this meeting. A sliver of guilt nagged at his insides when he thought of his newly found half-sister marrying the duke. Although, if you didn't take into account his injuries, the gentleman had much to offer. He seemed affable. He was rich and would no doubt take excellent care of Penelope, at least when it came to finances. And if they were intimate in the dark, Penelope could pretend the duke was a whole man. Thomas tensed. What a bastard he was. If he accepted the duke's offer, Penelope may never forgive him.

"Welcome, Newbury. Please have a seat." Thomas tried not to stare at the young duke as he awkwardly maneuvered into the room and onto the soft leather chair, using his cane and swinging his leg wide as it didn't bend at the knee. Then sitting awkwardly with his lame leg out straight. *He is a war hero; he deserves my respect and admiration.*

"Thank you for seeing me. I believe you know why I'm here."

Obviously, the duke wasn't one for mincing words. Wanting to get right down to negotiations. "Yes. I have an idea, but please enlighten me."

HARRY HAD SPENT little time in Wentworth's company, but he knew about him. After taking over the title, when his ne'er-do-well of a father had died, Wentworth did everything he could to unlink his family name from scandal and the gossip sheets. Wasn't easy since Wentworth had quite the reputation for the ladies and was known to the mamas as a rakehell and a poor one at that. Harry could only imagine how it pained Wentworth's self-respect to bow down to the parents of young debutants hoping to marry into a fortune. How fortunate for Wentworth the tides changed, and he found his American Heiress.

Wentworth could be a hard man, but a fair man. And he loved his wife. One un-redeeming quality Harry could overlook. Openly admitting to loving one's wife was embarrassing as far as Harry thought. He had no delusions of falling in love with Penelope. He was not capable of love.

"I have come to ask for Penelope's hand in marriage." He nearly choked on the words. Words he never thought he would utter. Damn Prinny for insisting the Sinclair line continue with his offspring. He'd be happy to grow old and die alone.

"I gathered that." Wentworth stood and went to his sideboard. "Would you care for some brandy?" He placed two glasses on his desk, picked up a square crystal decanter, and splashed amber liquid into one glass, paused and raised his brow awaiting the reply.

"Yes. Please. Thank you."

The duke poured his glass, walked around his desk, and handed it to him. "I have a great supplier; this is the best brandy in England." Instead of sitting back down at his desk, he leaned against the dark wood, savoring his drink.

After taking a sip, Harry had to agree to the fine quality of the liquor. "Smooth, goes down easy with a slow burn in the belly. If you would share the name of your supplier, I would be forever grateful."

Wentworth chuckled. "I'll have a case sent to your residence. Now let us get down to the business at hand. Lady Penelope has a sizable dowry. Since you appear to be financially solvent, I want half set aside for pin money and the rest invested for her future." The man stared into the amber liquid thoughtfully, then looked at Harry. Really looked at him, and he had to fight the urge to fidget. Wentworth was no fool, and Harry would have to be careful when he stepped out as Sinclair, lest he figure out they were one and the same. And he planned on stepping out as Hugh at all the upcoming social events. Starting tonight at the home of Lord and Lady Malden. A small, intimate affair with dancing. Harry could hardly wait to have Penelope in his arms for a waltz again. Even if he had to play at being his pretend cousin.

"Agreed."

"I will post the banns in a sennight to give my sister time to adjust to being betrothed to you, and I will send out invitations to a betrothal party in Lady Penelope and your honor in a fortnight. When, pray tell, will the ceremony take place?"

Harry hadn't thought that far in advance. Could he get away with a long engagement? Or should he tie the parson's noose soon and get it over with? The latter would be less painful for all. Especially Penelope as he couldn't imagine how stressful it would be being engaged to him of all people. "Soon. I will leave all the details up to you and your sister." As Harry reached for his cane, his hand fumbled, and the cane clattered to the floor. Wentworth stepped forward. Harry held up his hand to stop him. "I can manage." He leaned forward, his fingers reaching out until he contacted hard wood, curled his hand around the handle, pulled it close, and maneuvered to a standing position. "One more thing, Wentworth. Will Lady Penelope be attending the ball at Malden House this evening?"

"Yes."

"Splendid. My cousin, Mr. Hugh Sinclair, will be in attendance. I will ask him to pay his respects to Lady Penelope on my behalf as I'll not be attending." He bowed stiffly, one leg straight out to the side. Harry fought a smirk. It always amused him to play the cripple. Not that it was amusing as it made him feel sorry for anyone who was truly crippled. "Good day, Duke."

Wentworth bowed. "Good day to you, Newbury."

Two things Harry had needed to accomplish today were done. He spent the rest of the day at the offices of the War Secretary. Only half his mind payed attention to the conversation going on around the meeting table. The other half was on Penelope and tonight's ball.

# CHAPTER 4

"YOU KNEW THIS DAY WOULD COME," WENTWORTH SAID AS HE frowned at Penelope.

Her brother had called her down to his study and gave her the news. Her insides quivered at hearing she was to marry the Duke of Newbury. Truthfully, she didn't know how she felt. It relieved part of her that the entire shopping for a husband was over. The other part was frightened out of her mind at the thought of her wedding night and all the nights after.

The days would be easy. Most gentlemen slept late and attended clubs in the evenings. They spent very little time at home in the company of their wife. But the nights when he came home stinking of liquor and wanted his legal rights as a husband had her heart beating in despair. Perhaps his injuries rendered him incapable of performing his husbandly duties. *I can hope, can't I?*

"Yes. I did. But I was hoping for more time." Her voice sounded distant to her own ears.

"Newbury has the reputation of being an exemplary man. There are no rumors of him treating his mistress with anything but generosity and kindness. If I believed he would treat you any differently, I would not have agreed to this marriage."

Her heart stopped. So, he could perform in the marriage bed. But perhaps he loved his mistress and wouldn't want to bed her. She knew it was false hope. He was a duke and needed heirs, and she was the only one who could give him them. "When will the ceremony take place?" Truthfully, she didn't care. The sooner the better, so she could get her wedding night over with. A nagging in the back of her mind rang out. Will the duke be disappointed with me?

"You and Emma can begin planning. Two months' time should be sufficient. A minor affair, family and close friends at Stoney Brook Manor. The ceremony in the small chapel on the grounds. Does that agree with you?"

Did it? And did her input really have any bearings on Thomas's already made decisions? Did she really even care? She should be so grateful for Wentworth and his taking her into his home as his sister. It wasn't that she wasn't. She was eternally grateful. Without him, she would be destitute in the English countryside, forced to do unspeakable things to stay alive. If she'd been fortunate, a well-to-do country gentleman would have made her his wife. If she'd been unfortunate, she'd have been forced to sell her body. Her self-respect. Her soul. Her stomach churned at the thought.

"I know I've told you before, Thomas, but thank you for rescuing me. I don't know how long I could've hidden from Hadley. I'm trying to be positive about this marriage and not dwell on the duke's shortcomings. I will be the Duchess of Newbury, which means absolutely nothing to me. To you and the members of the ton, it means a great deal. I will try to make you proud. Be worthy of the title of duchess. Be a loyal and kind wife to the duke. Make him never regret his decision to marry me." She paused thoughtfully. "Why is he marrying me? My birth is scandalous and my upbringing less than stellar. I'm convinced there are mamas of debutants willing to throw their daughters at the duke, even crippled as he is? So why me?"

Wentworth pulled on his collar and cleared his throat, clearly uncomfortable with the way the conversation had turned. "The only person who knows the answer to the question is Newbury. Perhaps you should ask him?"

She fought down her nervous laughter trying to escape. "Perhaps I will broach the subject someday but not anytime soon. Do you mind if I retire to my room and rest before tonight's ball?"

"You may go." He looked thoughtful. "One thing, Newbury is not attending this evening, but his cousin, Mr. Hugh Sinclair, will be. Expect him to pay homage to you."

Homage to her? What did that mean. Why wasn't Newbury attending? She'd much rather spend the night in his company and get to know him better since they would wed soon. The time she spent scandalously waltzing in Mr. Sinclair's arms haunted her dreams. Harry's face as a pirate and Hugh's mask covered face blurred together in her dreams and became one unsettling her. She had woken up several nights lately in a sweat-soaked night rail and a scream on her lips.

AS THE COACH CARRYING WENTWORTH, Emma, and Penelope finally pulled up beneath the portico of Malden House after waiting in the endless queue of carriages, Penelope's stomach rolled with unease. It would be the first time that she would be introduced and attending a society ball. Emma had warned her the gossips' tongues would wag fast and often tonight. However, Wentworth would dare anyone to disrespect her in his presence. If only her insides would settle down because she was terrified of these people. She followed Wentworth and Emma up the grand staircase to the receiving line and tried to recall all Emma told her would occur. What happened was a servant bellowed in a loud voice, "The Duke and Duchess of Wentworth and Lady Penelope Seabrook."

Her breath held inside her lungs as she waited for someone, anyone, to contradict the title of lady before her name. No one did, although it became uncomfortably quiet on the landing. Wentworth motioned her forward, not giving her time to dwell on the quiet and said, "Lord and Lady Malden may I present Lady Penelope Seabrook, my sister."

Penelope curtsied. "Lord and Lady Malden, it's a pleasure to make your acquaintance."

Lady Malden, an attractive woman of later years, smiled warmly at her. "Welcome to our home, Lady Penelope."

"Thank you."

"Yes, welcome," Lord Malden said in a booming voice.

"That went well," Wentworth whispered as he escorted his wife and sister, each on one arm, into the warmly lit ballroom already full to bursting with bodies. As all eyes looked their way, conversation paused throughout the room. Her brother stiffened beside her and glared at the room, daring anyone to be rude to her. Slowly the conversations picked up again, and everyone went about their business. Penelope inhaled in much-needed air and breathed, "Thank you."

Wentworth looked at her, his features tense, then changed before her eyes to relaxed, and he grinned. "You're welcome. I did what any dutiful brother would do. Aye, this must be Mr. Hugh Sinclair coming this way as he resembles Newbury."

Her eyes fell upon the gentleman slowly making his way toward them, and her insides tumbled at the uncanny resemblance to Newbury. Well, to the Duke of Newbury's good side. Not to mention the height and build. He looked more like Newbury's brother than a cousin. Since the night she'd met him, he had a mask on, she was seeing his face for the first time. He had the same dark hair and deep blue eyes. He was dressed in formal wear, and goose bumps broke out on her exposed flesh as she recalled her waltz with him. How he'd held her improperly close and said intimate things to her.

Her eyes were riveted to his face as he smiled. "Your Graces, Lady Penelope. Newbury asked if I would introduce myself so I may be of assistance tonight in any way possible." He bowed quite dramatically. "Mr. Hugh Sinclair at your service."

Wentworth nodded his head. "Yes, Newbury told me you would be in attendance. How unfortunate he wasn't able to attend himself."

Mr. Sinclair's eyes dimmed. "Yes. Unfortunate indeed."

"Duchess, Lady Penelope, may I present Mr. Hugh Sinclair."

Emma curtsied, lifted up her white gloved hand and Mr. Sinclair took it, bowing over it. "It's a pleasure to make your acquaintance, Mr. Sinclair."

"The pleasure is all mine, Your Grace."

He turned, bowed her way, making Penelope drop into a curtsy. "Nice to see you again, Mr. Sinclair." His eyes sparkled as he looked his fill at her, and she shivered with awareness. Awareness he should not be making her experience.

"The pleasure is all mine, I assure you. Could you please pencil me in for the first waltz of the evening?"

"She has not been given permission from the Patronesses at Almack's to waltz yet." The duchess replied on Penelope's behalf. "Perhaps another dance?"

"Yes. Perhaps another," Sinclair said.

"Yes, another." Penelope's cheeks were aflame. The attraction she'd felt for Mr. Sinclair the other night and now on a higher level needed to stop since she was affianced to his cousin. Did Newbury know what a charming flirt his cousin was? Because surely the man was daft putting her in Mr. Sinclair's care. Perhaps he was testing her loyalty? If so, she planned on passing. She could bury her attraction. She had to, and she would. She may be all of seventeen, but she'd learned long ago to hide her feelings from the world. Being a servant along with her mother in a degenerate's house forced one to hide what was inside. Viscount Hadley thrived on fear, so she'd learned to hide it and all other emotions. Deadened them inside.

As her mind wandered, she caught pieces of the conversation between Wentworth, Emma, and Sinclair. Weather, Parliament, Wigs, Tories, things she cared little for. All she'd cared about before coming to London was surviving. Some things were hard to change. She still needed to survive. The difference was the jungle had changed to include much more dangerous beings.

Music had never been a part of her life, not until her dancing lessons, but even she recognized the first strings of a waltz after several country reels concluded. Relief and disappointment washed over her at not being able to dance the waltz.

"Milady." Mr. Sinclair bowed. "Since the waltz is forbidden, would you care to take a turn around the room?" He held out his arm. Penelope placed her arm on his, and he escorted her around the outer fringes of the dancefloor but in front of all the chairs. Chairs with people watching and gossiping. "I believe congratulations are in order for your upcoming nuptials to my cousin."

Her steps faulted, but he steadied her and they

continued walking as if nothing happened. "Yes. Thank you. I hope he told you the bands won't be posted until next week?"

"Yes. Don't worry, your secret is safe with me. I wouldn't dream of spoiling the ton's surprise."

"Thank you."

"Is there anything I can tell you about Newbury? He gave me permission to ease your concerns if you have any." His voice was light. His lips were smiling, but his eyes darkened with a hint of worry.

Did she have concerns? What newly betrothed would not when marrying a perfect stranger. An injured stranger with one eye, a painful-looking scar, and a leg that didn't work properly. Besides the fact he held the title of duke, he wasn't much of a prize. But then again, she wasn't either. No, indeed, she was no prize. "Part of me has questions, part of me doesn't."

He lead her towards French doors. "Let us get some air, and you can ask away whatever you want with no one overhearing."

Before she could protest to being in private with him, they passed thru the open doors and stepped out onto the terrace. He led her to a darkened corner overlooking dimly lit gardens where several people milled around. Mr. Sinclair leaned his back against a wrought-iron railing, his legs casually crossed at the ankle and his arms across his fine chest. The man exuded relaxation as though he hadn't a care in the world. Unless one looked deep into his eyes to see the wariness. Strange. What did Mr. Sinclair have to be wary about as they discussed his cousin?

Facing him, she toyed with her fan, which had been wrapped around her wrist. "I'm at a loss."

One side of his mouth tipped up, making him look devilishly handsome and dangerous. Dangerous because she didn't want to play whatever game he was playing. It was clear he was up to something.

"I presume you are wondering if he can perform his husbandly duties because of his injuries."

Mortified at his words, she gasped and turned to leave. His hand reached out, curled around her upper arm to stop her. Ignoring the heat of the contact and the warmth of her cheeks, she turned back and tried to think of a scathing remark. Her tongue, however, refused to work.

"Please forgive me. That was uncalled for. A gentleman never says such things to an innocent. I find myself, for the first time since Newbury sustained his injuries, envious of him." Stepping closer to her, he cupped her chin, tilted her head up, forcing her to look directly into his dark blue eyes. "I find I want what he has. To my dismay, I find myself wanting you."

She swallowed, her pulse hammering inside her body to go along with her beating heart. Not to mention, her insides fluttered with what she believed was desire. Having never felt it before, she couldn't know for certain.

"I want one kiss. Just one, may I?"

Penelope couldn't breathe, nor could she move. She'd fallen completely under this man's spell. What a horrible person she was to be wanting a kiss from the cousin of her betrothed. Where had her honor and respect gone? She may have been brought up differently than anyone else in attendance tonight, but her mother instilled honor and respect in her. Not only respect for others but herself as well.

Kissing Mr. Sinclair displayed neither of those attributes. Looking into his eyes, which had darkened with what she recognized as want, need, and desire had the tip of her tongue running across her lips as they'd become parched. The thumping of her heart near deafening. She inhaled gently and held it inside her lungs as the anticipation dragged on and on. Did the man not mean to prepare her for his lips. Just as she planned to step back and give up, his breath skated across her lips. His mouth so close to hers she felt the heat.

"Forgive me." He stepped back and bowed. "I find I can't disrespect Newbury, or you." Stunned speechless, her eyes bored a hole through his back as he retreated inside the ballroom. She gasped, dragging in much-needed air into her lungs. Her hand gripped the iron railing as she continued to breathe in and out, in and out. Part of her was relieved Mr. Sinclair didn't kiss her. If he had, it would plague her with guilt. And the next time she was in the Duke of Newbury's company, she would not be able to look him in the eye. Yes. It was a good thing he didn't kiss her. Her fingers touched her still trembling lips and the not so quite proper part of her wished for the kiss. His honorable actions had her wanting him more. Wanting one man and marrying another. Attracted to both men in unique ways. What a dilemma her young self had fallen into.

Once her nerves settled down, she entered the ballroom, her eyes seeking her family or a friend. Too bad she had no friends. Someone to help her forget what almost transpired out on the terrace. Just as she was giving up hope, she spotted Emma and Bella, sitting together looking as though they were gossiping about someone or something. She forced herself to stroll slowly halfway around the ballroom so as to not draw attention to herself. When she really wanted was to hike up her skirts and run. Something she could not do unless she wanted to cause even more of a scandal than she already had just by being present tonight.

Finally she arrived at their side, dropped into the vacant seat next to Bella, and sighed.

"Where have you been?" Emma asked as she sipped champagne and nibbled on a biscuit. I was ready to find Thomas and have him search for you."

"Yes," Bella said with a sparkle in her eyes and a beautiful smile on her equally beautiful face. "Where have you been? Did Mr. Sinclair steal a private moment with you? Which would be most improper seeing's how you are affianced to his cousin. But I must admit, he cuts a dashing figure and his face is mighty handsome. If either of you repeat this, I'll deny it. I can't have Myles thinking there is any gentleman more handsome than he."

Penelope didn't know what to say. Did she confide in the ladies or keep her secrets to herself? Perhaps if she explained what happened, they could advise her what to do if she found herself alone with Mr. Sinclair again.

"I have something to say. But you each must promise me it goes no further. Don't give me the line you have no secrets from your husbands because that's not true. Everyone has secrets."

Bella and Emma both agreed to secrecy.

"Before I continue, I want you to know that nothing happened. Mr. Sinclair and I went out on the veranda. He said Newbury gave him permission to answer questions I may have about him. I couldn't come up with any."

"Perhaps it would be better to ask His Grace if you have anything you want to know," Emma said right before she finished the last of her biscuit.

"I agree with Emma," Bella said. "He may have given his cousin permission to answer your questions, but I would bet my next month's pin money on Newbury wanting you to ask him yourself."

"That's not all." Penelope prepared herself for a scolding. She was, after all, only ten and seven. Even if there were days she felt years older, body and mind. "He said for the first time since the duke's injuries, he envies him."

"Why?" Bella and Emma asked simultaneously.

"Because he finds himself attracted to me and wants to kiss me."

Emma gasped and quickly covered her mouth to hide the noise. Her blue eyes, however, went big as a teacup's saucer. Bella raised one perfect blonde brow.

"He didn't. We didn't," Penelope blurted out.

"Thank goodness," Emma said as she used her hands to smooth her skirts. "What were you thinking going out onto the veranda with him alone? If you'd been caught, scandal would have you marrying him instead of the duke."

Breathe, Penelope, breathe. Half of her wanted to ask, would that be so terribly wrong? The other half knew better. "I'm sorry. If Wentworth knew he would keep me under lock and key until the wedding. And the duke, he'd be shocked and disappointed. There would be no need for Wentworth to lock me up because there'd be no wedding. What a disgrace I am to the Seabrook family. Wentworth should send me back, hence where I came from."

Bella touched her hand. "Don't be a silly goose. Wentworth will never know. What's done is done and luckily you came through it unscathed and without scandal. Don't temp fate another time, though. You may not be so fortunate."

"I agree with what Bella said," Emma chimed in. You must remain above reproach. I realize the Seabrook family, even before I arrived in England, didn't always behave in a stellar manner, my husband had a dreadful reputation for being a rakehell and seducing young widows. The previous duke, your father, well you know about his scandalous past. Bella, stringing along two gentlemen. Amelia having," she lowered her voice to a whisper, "Olivia out of wedlock. Even if she'd given herself to her betrothed only a week before his tragic death and their planned wedding."

"Not to mention," Bella interjected, "Sebastian and Thomas fighting over you. Such scandal indeed."

"Please explain, with details, everything you just told me." How had Penelope heard none of this before? She certainly came from an interesting family. And thank God she did. And she loved each and every one of them.

"Not now," Emma said. "Perhaps another time when we have privacy. Also, my husband and yours, Bella, are coming this way. I believe it's time to go."

ONCE AT HOME, in her room dressed in her night rail and matching robe, Penelope lay on the chaise in front of the roaring fire beneath a throw. Sleep eluded her, so she'd gotten out of bed and moved to the chaise. Her mind was swirling with thoughts and memories of the evening. One moment guilt bombarded her and the next memories of the emotions Mr. Sinclair awoke inside her, pushing aside her strange attraction to Newbury.

Tears slid down her cheeks. What a terrible person she'd become. After tonight, how could she go through with her nuptials to Newbury? She worried because secrets had a way of being revealed. What if in a moment of anger, Mr. Sinclair told Harry about their almost kiss? What if Harry called him out? Surely, he couldn't win a duel against his cousin. His death would be on her conscience forever. The future of all three of them ruined. More than ruined for Newbury. He'd be dead. How could she live with herself if that came to pass?

No. The only way to solve this issue was to admit to the Duke of Newbury the truth. That his cousin and she had private words on the veranda alone and almost kissed. No. That would be worse. He definitely would call Mr. Sinclair out. What a dilemma. How did she fix this? Perhaps the only thing she could do was stay silent. Confessing to the duke would cause a rift between the cousins. For the sake of all parties, she would remain silent and deal with the guilt gnawing at her insides.

Sometimes being a member of the Seabrook family was too hard. One always had to be at one's best.

Think before you speak, lest you embarrass yourself or a family member, or God forbid cause a scandal.

Always use the correct utensil when eating.

Sip your tea, do not slurp.

Do not wear a day dress in the evening.

Never, ever, leave the house without gloves and a hat.

Do not address a duke as a lord or an earl as your grace.

And the list went on and on. How was she to remember it all and not misstep or misspeak? She couldn't blame Wentworth for bringing her to London. She'd sent a letter asking for his help. If only she could go back in time and find another way.

Never to have sent the letter and become a burden on Wentworth and the rest of his family.

Never to have met the duke or his cousin.

She sighed, and more tears escaped her eyes. If she'd met none of them, her heart ached at the thought, she'd have missed out on ever having known such wonderful, caring, and loving people. Oh dear, her lungs burned. Closing her eyes, she wished for sleep. Dreamless, peaceful sleep so she could wake up in the morning fresh and ready to handle anything or anyone that came her way.

AFTER LEAVING THE BALL, Harry took his unmarked carriage to his ex-mistress's house. His driver knew to drop him off a block away, and he made his way silently in the night.

Knowing to expect him, she greeted him at the back door under the blackness of night dressed in a her night clothes, her long auburn tresses down and brushed to a high sheen. Rose Albright was comely. He'd known her most of his life. Her mother had served in his father's home and then she had. After his father and uncle's deaths and Harry left the army she'd arrived in London on his doorstep asking for employment. She'd served as a maid for a time, before she became his mistress. Harry had turned down her offer of being his mistress from the beginning. Fought it for several months as she worked as a downstairs maid in his home. Until one night, she somehow knew the demons from war visited him in the dark of night, and she'd come to him and offered her body.

Thinking back now, he wasn't proud of himself for given in to his sexual urges. She hadn't been a virgin but that didn't lessen the responsibility he felt for her and refused to allow her to continue on as a maid in his home. He Rented her a small residence and provided her with a lady companion. Rose was his mistress for the better part of a year. When the year ended things gradually changed. Their sexual relationship ended and they became friends. He still felt responsible for her and his support continued.

"Something is bothering you, Harry. Please join me in the parlor by the warm hearth, and I'll pour you a brandy."

Rose was the only person, other than those he worked with, who knew about his work with the War Office. He trusted her with his life. After dropping his weary body onto the settee and taking the offered drink, he stretched his legs out and sighed. Rose sat beside him and covered them both with a throw.

"So tell me what has you upset. And don't say nothing. I know you too well." She rested her head on his shoulder, and the sound of her even breathing traveled to his ears.

"I don't know where to begin. Before you read it in the London Times, I offered for Lady Penelope Seabrook's hand in marriage. Her brother accepted."

"I see."

"There is one more thing I'd like to talk to you about. Please keep an open mind and know I'm doing what I believe is right for you." He stretched his arm around her back and hugged her close.

"I'm giving you a dowry, and I've written Mr. George Heatherford from Lancaster."

"What…" She gasped and pulled out from beneath his arm. He tugged her back.

"Let me finish. George and I served together under Wellington. I trust him with my life, and I have. Just as he trusted his life to me. We served as brothers. If I could choose anyone in England to be my brother, I would choose him. George is the youngest son of a Marquess. Has lands and is working those lands. He needs and wants a wife who has no aspirations of becoming a Marchioness as he has five older brothers. He is a fine and honorable man and most of the ladies find him handsome. I have invited him to visit. He arrives the day after tomorrow." Harry waited for some sound from Rose besides the sound of her crying and sniffling.

After a time, she said in a soft sad tone, "I understand why you are doing this. You won't keep a mistress or an ex-mistress once you marry so you're finding a worthy man who can and will take care of me. But why would Mr. Heatherford agree to this arrangement? I'm soiled goods."

He never thought of her as soiled goods. He preferred to look at it as though she were widowed. And Heatherford, as a younger son, understood the plight of those less fortunate. It really did not differ from any arranged married. There were no guarantees the lady was pure and untouched.

Honestly, Harry wasn't brought up within the privilege of the ton so it didn't matter to him. Harry had explained the whole situation to Heatherford, and he didn't take offense to Rose's plight. She intrigued him. And he knew if Harry cared enough about her to secure a wonderful future for her, then she was worthy of being his wife.

"Please never utter those words again. We have loved each other for many years, as friends, then lovers, then back to friends, and there is no shame in giving yourself to someone you love." He turned and cupped her cheeks with his hands, his fingers swiping at her tears. "Whether or not you believe it, you saved me from myself. I'd been broken in body and soul when I returned from war and became a duke. I couldn't sleep, or when I did I had awful nightmares, which made me afraid to sleep. I had no appetite. I didn't socialize, nor leave my new home, unless I really had to for work." He swallowed the lump in his throat. "You brought me back. Your kindness, compassion, understanding, and love saved me. You do not understand how close I came many times to taking my life. Living had become too painful until you.

"My friend is honored that I thought of him. He knows how much you mean to me, and he is eager to make your acquaintance so you two can start your lives together. I believe in my heart you will come to love him and he you. Please agree to meet him and give this a chance?"

Rose had known she could not remain with Harry forever. Not once he became a duke. She'd spent most of her life around him. Her mother had been a maid in his father's house. She'd been born there, educated there, and then served Harry's father after her mother passed. When Harry's father died, she'd traveled to Harry and begged for employment. As a youthful girl and a young woman, she'd had a secret crush on him.

It pained her heart to leave him. She loved him. When they first came together in the bedroom, there'd been passion. That passion eventually turned to a deep abiding love of friendship and a comfortability of intimacy. She knew one day they would part. As much as she loved him, she knew he would marry another. Him becoming a duke only solidified that for her. However, if he hadn't planned to ever send her away, she would have stayed until death separated them. She owed him everything. He was marrying a lady of dubious birth, even though she was the half-sister of a duke, she was still a bastard. As Rose was. They had that in common. Her mother went to her grave pretending to be a widow, but Rose knew the truth. And so did Harry. He never cared. As far as it concerned her, there would never be a more honorable man than Harry. Lady Penelope was the luckiest woman in the world. And she was second.

His warm, large hands still cupped her face and his beautiful blue eyes, laced with concern, never looked away from her green ones. "I knew one day we would part," she said. "Please don't feel bad for me. I look forward to meeting Mr. Heatherford. If you sing his praises, they should be sung. I need not think about marrying him. I will." There was no stopping as a new flood of tears dripped down her cheeks only to be absorbed by his hands. "Never feel guilty about this. I am happy for you and as much as it breaks my heart to move on, I will. Knowing we are both doing the right thing makes it easier." She pushed his hands away and forced herself to be strong. "I will see you to the door." Once there, she handed him his greatcoat and hat. "Please tell Mr. Heatherford when he arrives that I am packed and ready to travel to his home." She gulped in air around the blockage in her raw throat. "I think it's best if we say goodbye now. I pray

Penelope understands what a good man you are. And can love you for your strengths as well as your weaknesses." She rose on her toes for one last kiss.

The door closed behind Harry and she slid to the floor, hugging her knees to her chest, and sobbed.

"I'm sorry, child." Mrs. Dinmore, her companion, a kind, plump woman in her forties with no family to speak of, joined her on the ground and hugged her tightly. "I know saying goodbye wasn't easy. He is one of the finest men. Forgive me for eavesdropping, but this Mr. Heatherford sounds like a right fine man himself. I always worried about your future when the duke took a wife. I can worry no more."

After Rose's sobs quieted down and she found her voice, she asked, "Will you come with me? I don't think I can manage without you?"

"Nonsense, child, you will manage fine. The splendid news is you won't have to manage alone. If it's agreeable with Mr. Heatherford, I will stay in your employ, or rather your soon-to-be husband's employ until you no longer need me."

"I'll always need you, Mrs. Dinmore, always."

"Now that that's settled, let's get you into bed. You'll catch your death here on the icy floor. We have much to do in the next few days. What with packing and then traveling to your new home." Mrs. Dinmore helped her stand up. "I have pleasant feelings about this new chapter in your life. Yes, indeed, good feelings."

# CHAPTER 5

AFTER HE ARRIVED HOME, HARRY SAT IN A COMFORTABLE chair, his feet on an ottoman in the library with a brandy cradled in his hand. After the time he spent at the ball with Penelope, and then with Rose, sleep would never come to him tonight. So why bother trying. Two things plagued him. First, Penelope. He'd not meant to get her alone and nearly pull her into an embrace and kiss her. Oh, he wanted to. But as Harry, not Hugh. He didn't want to confuse her and cause her any undo guilt. It would take all of his strength not to act on his emotions.

When he looked deep into her eyes out on the veranda, he found himself lost in her silvery blue ones. It was as though she'd cast a spell on him since the very first night they met at Mr. Stuart Spencer's home. He'd known Spencer hadn't invited him there for his sister, Mary. Spencer had invited him so Wentworth could introduce him to Penelope. Deduce whether he would make a favorable match with her. And, no doubt, to find out for himself if the rumors about his disfigurement were true. From that very night, he thought about her. What her lips would taste and feel like. Soft and sweet, no doubt. What her body would feel like beneath his roaming hands. Warm and supple, most definitely.

What her laughter would sound like. What little noises would she make when he made love to her and brought her pleasure. And what it would feel like to be inside her, taking them both to unimaginable pleasures and beyond.

Instead, now that he was home, he realized what a mistake he made with her this evening. Because when she found out the truth about him, she would hate him and never trust him again. She would feel like he made a fool of her. Which was never his intentions. Never that. He'd not been thinking beyond spending time with her. Private time so she would let her emotions and personality out instead of trying to be a good lady of the ton. Neither of them grew up within the confines of the ton's rules. When they married, he hoped she would be her true self. When out in society, he expected her to act as a proper duchess, but in the privacy of their bedchamber and home, he wanted the real Penelope. The genuine girl behind the mask her brother made her wear at all times. That girl intrigued him, not that he didn't like the refined Penelope, he just thought he'd like the unrefined one just as well, or even more. God knew, he wasn't all that refined himself. Spending time in the army in battle had one realizing Society's rules and following them didn't make you a better person. One could be the best person in the world and not have a title, money, or lands. Being a member of the ton didn't keep one safe from the enemy. A bullet fell a member of the aristocracy as easily as it fell a man of the lower classes.

Harry continued to work for the War Office, not because he had to, because he wanted to. Felt compelled to. Had this ingrained need to do the right thing. To find those responsible for injustices and make them pay. Not out of vengeance —out of honor. Men like the Baron Littleton who cost many soldiers and civilians, women and children their lives needed to pay for his crimes. Even now he was plotting the death of King George III and the Prince Regent. The man had no conscience. And it was up to Harry and the rest of the loyal people he worked with to protect the crown and innocent people from those wanting to do harm.

His hand rubbed his chest, hoping to ease the pain. He put his untouched glass of brandy down on the table beside his chair and stretched out, trying to ease the stiffness in his joints. The war had done damage to his body. Having been shot several times, he still had fragments of bullets lodged inside his thigh and shoulder. Nothing the surgeons could do about it. He wasn't complaining, not when he witnessed bloody carnage all around him, leaving the ground littered with dead bodies as far as the eye could see. No. He would never complain. Actually, living in constant pain reminded him how lucky he was to be alive, and that kept him moving forward.

After the Napoleonic Wars, reading and meditation and Rose had kept him sane. If it wasn't for those three, he would've given up on life and humanity. You can't go to war and return without your perspective on life being altered.

Before the war, he never gave much thought to food, shelter, medicine, or physicians. All readily available to him in the country growing up with his father. Not always during fighting. He had not been a duke during the war. If he had, he would've had certain accommodations and privileges. Being a member of the peerage gave one privileges, not so if you weren't. Sometimes the supplies didn't reach them, and they went hungry and cold. And always tired and weary to the bone. But when the enemy came calling, you mustered up the energy and courage to fight. Fight for your country and king. Fight to live.

When he returned, his staff helped him adjust to being a

duke. His meditation and reading helped him heal inside and out. He had no choice but to heal. He had people relying on him. He had that in the army with those who served under him. He had it now, only different, but still the goal was to stay alive and prosper.

There was no denying the progress of time and change. Not with the end of the war. Not with industrial changes. Not with Parliament. His eyes closed, and he sighed with a weary heart and overtired mind. He needed several hours of sleep. Fortunately for him, he got them.

MORNING FOUND Penelope curled up on her chaise, shivering as her maid, Clarisse, came in to open the drapes and assist her in dressing. Even though the fire had been stoked earlier, the room held a chill, and she burrowed beneath the throw. How could it be morning when she was more exhausted now than last night?

"Will the moss green day dress be to your liking, milady?"

"Yes." Penelope dragged herself up and behind the privacy screen to perform her morning ablutions.

Dressed and her hair done up, Penelope made her way down the stairs and into the warm, yellow breakfast room. The sun shined unusually bright today, and she leaned against one of the tall windows and basked in the warmth from the rays.

"Good morning, Penelope," Emma said as she entered the room, yawning and looking slightly mussed—no doubt having come from the nursery and dealing with her two adorable boys. An heir and a spare. Even with her hair falling out of its coiffeur and her clothes wrinkled, Emma was truly beautiful. Her blonde hair, thick and wavy, her eyes a bright blue and her skin, creamy and smooth. They made a striking couple as Wentworth had similar blue eyes and blond hair. And the love they shared had her envious and wondering if she would have that with Harry? Then she remembered what had transpired between, or had not transpired between, Mr. Sinclair and her. Last evening had her stomach spinning and her cheeks heating with mortification.

She needed to speak with Emma more about it. About what a horrible person she was. Just as she spoke, Wentworth swept into the room dressed in brown riding clothes and bringing the chill from the outside with him. "Morning. The sun is shining. Myles and I went for a ride in Hyde Park. Nothing like a fast ride through the park to get one's blood flowing." He kissed Emma on the forehead. "How is my duchess this morning? You were fast asleep when I left."

"I'm well. The boys were up early and I spent time with them while they ate breakfast." She patted her hair. "Although I think some of their oats and mashed apples ended up in my hair." She laughed. "Now I'm going to enjoy my food and chocolate." She heaped her plate to overflowing from the sideboard, and a footman assisted her in sitting.

Wentworth made himself a plate and took the seat at the opposite end of the table. "Are you going to stand at the window all morning?"

Inhaling and exhaling, Penelope made her way to the sideboard and added coddled eggs, sausages, fruit, and pastry to her plate and waved off the footman. She could seat herself. He quickly came over with warm chocolate, and Penelope cradled the china cup in her hands.

"I received a missive this morning from Newbury asking permission to take you for a turn around the park this afternoon at four."

Four. The "to see and be seen" hour. Taking a sip of chocolate, she willed her insides to remain calm. It wouldn't do to cast up her accounts at the breakfast table. Was she ready for all of London to know about her and Newbury? Was she ready to be in his company alone, but in public? With all eyes of the ton on them? No time like today to get used to spending time with him. After all, they would be married soon enough. And she would spend all eternity with him.

"I'll go. The sooner people know about us, the easier it will be next week when the banns are posted. It's just…"

"What?" Both Wentworth and Emma said in unison.

What indeed? "It's just that I've only been living here a short time. I feel as though I've only just gotten to know you both and soon I'll be wed to the Duke of Newbury and gone." She really fought hard not to cry, but those infernal tears came anyway. Embarrassed by them, she used her hand to wipe them off her cheeks, only it proved useless as more tears kept replacing them. "Forgive me, I don't mean to cry. I've never been a watering pot, but lately…"

Emma reached out and placed her hand on Penelope's. "It's quite all right, Penelope. In some ways I know how you feel. When my papa died and Wentworth came to Boston and took me across the Atlantic Ocean to England and thrust me into his family, I too felt unsettled, lost, and remember crying myself to sleep many nights. It certainly didn't help when Sebastian and Wentworth fought over me. Sebastian stormed out of the house, and we didn't see him for nearly two years. I believed it was my fault and feared his mother and sisters would hate me.

"Thankfully, they didn't and were pleased when Thomas and I wed. However, all the changes occurring in my life at the time left me sad. My papa had died, I lived in a foreign country, and it appalled most of the ton when Thomas married me, his American ward. You, my dear, are still grieving for your mother and settling in with your new family. But I promise you, we will see each other often. The duke's London townhome is within walking distance. Getting married will not take you away from us."

As Emma spoke, Penelope realized their situations were similar. The kind and compassionate words had more tears pooling in her eyes. For the first of many times since she arrived in London, Penelope was very thankful for the tolerance and kindness of her natural father's family. God knew her father had no kindness for her or her mother. How such a horrible man sired such wonderful people proved a mystery. Until her dying breath, she would be forever grateful. "Thank you." Between the tears clogging her throat and the heaviness in her heart, no other words would come through her lips. "If you'll excuse me, I will retire to the drawing room and work on my embroidery."

THE REST of the day passed quickly. Penelope, dressed in a navy-blue walking dress with cream spencer and half-kid boots, sat clutching a reticle that matched the cream of her spencer perfectly and waited in the drawing room for Newbury to arrive. Oh, and one must not forget her hat. A wide-brimmed affair in cream with navy ribbon tied beneath her chin in a perfect bow, thanks to her maid.

She looked and felt like a doll she'd seen in a store window on Bond Street recently. All dressed up with nowhere to go. Only Penelope had somewhere to go. And by the voices traveling down the hallway from the front foyer and the click of a cane on the wood floors, followed by a shuffle and step and repeat, her duke had arrived.

Emma whispered from her seat beside her on the settee, "Try to relax and get to know the duke. I have heard good things about the man."

"I will try." She shivered even though the drawing room was warm.

After greetings, bows, and curtsies were made, Newbury stood before her. "Shall we?"

She forced herself to smile. "We shall." After standing, she wrapped her arm around his and let him lead her down the hall, out the door, and down the stairs to an open phaeton.

Newbury assisted her into the high two-seater carriage she'd heard was dangerous.

After taking his seat beside her, he took the reins and set the phaeton in motion onto Park Ave as they made their way to Hyde Park. "You look worried. Don't be. I've been driving carriages for years. You've, no doubt, heard of the phaeton's reputation for being dangerous and easily tipping over. Only when a gentleman is hell bent on racing. You, my dear, are safe with me."

Safe with him? Was she really? She was marrying a stranger who behind closed doors could be a monster that had nothing to do with his damaged face and body. Growing up and then working for the vile viscount, she'd seen how bad humanity could be. Outwardly, Viscount Hadley appeared normal enough. The man had a wife and five children. Once you no longer looked inside the windows, but lived there, you met the demon inside the man. He beat his wife and children. Took liberties with most of the female staff. Used her mother repeatedly. Although Penelope knew she offered up herself so he would leave her alone. The viscount first touched her when she was around twelve. Nearly raped her. Did everything but take her maidenhead. After that one encounter, her mother stepped in and kept the reprobate occupied. Kept him away from her…mostly.

Even at that age Penelope wasn't naïve when it came to men and women and matters of the flesh.

"You are still looking worried. You don't trust me to keep you safe?"

≈

HARRY DIDN'T LIKE that Penelope looked frightened. Being with him out in the open, surrounded by a crush of carriages and both men and women on horseback, now that they'd entered the park, should have her at ease. What could he possibly do to her with all eyes on them? It would be remiss of him not to notice all the stares and whispers swirling around them. Because of his covert career, he was always aware of his surroundings. Just in case.

Hence, why he had two loaded pistols in his greatcoat pockets. The metal lion's head of his cane unscrewed and became the handle of a sword. Beneath the seat held several rifles, loaded and ready to fire.

He'd learned in the army to be ready for anything. When you least expect an attack, expect one. Of course, he wasn't in the army anymore, but still. One could never be too careful. His cover could be revealed. There already were rumors he worked for the Secretary of War. Any sane person would laugh and think it ridiculous, but not all. Being a spy put Penelope in danger. Once they wed, he would plan for two bodyguards to accompany her everywhere.

"Is it just me, or is everyone staring and whispering?" Penelope turned her head to look at him, sending his heart pounding at her blinding beauty.

"Yes. Let them enjoy themselves. Any moment another gossip worthy couple will come along and their attention will shift to them. We will be long forgotten." He lied, of course. They would spark gossip for some time to come. How could they not? A bastard daughter of a duke and a crippled, hideous duke to be joined in holy matrimony. Not something that happened in aristocracy every day. Probably never.

One side of her mouth quirked up. "Thank you for making light of it. But I'm too old to believe such nonsense."

"Forgive me."

"I forgive you." As she spoke the words, her hand drifted over his thigh, as though she were going to touch him. She gasped and pulled it back. Her cheeks reddened.

"You can touch me. I don't bite. At least not anymore. My nanny used to tell stories about me biting other children. Didn't last long once she put vile cleaning soap in my mouth each time I did."

Her giggles were music to Harry's ears. A ride in the park on a sunny, mild day should be void of tension and unease.

"How long have you been out of the army?"

"Since Waterloo. The army didn't need a cripple. I sold off my commission, came to London, and became a duke. A fairy tale ending." He sounded bitter, but he wasn't. Until she knew his secrets he had to make it all appear real.

"I'm sorry."

"Nothing to be sorry for." His nerves tightened with guilt. Deceiving her would have dire consequences for him soon. "Sinclair said he took a turn around the ballroom last evening with you. I hope he behaved himself."

Her cheeks reddened once again. "Yes, he was quite the gentleman."

"Glad to hear it." Harry pulled on the reins. His horse was getting antsy with the crawl of carriages on Rotten Row. Cinnamon wanted to stretch her legs. *I do too, girl, I do too. He told me he wanted to waltz with you, but you have not been given permission yet.*

"Will you ever dance again, Your Grace?" she asked in a soft voice shocking him with her question.

"Perhaps. But don't worry if you like to twirl around the

dance floor, Sinclair or some other gentleman will be available. You need not worry about missing out."

She gasped or coughed. Or coughed to hide her gasp. He'd bet on the latter. "I wasn't worried about putting away my dancing shoes. I was more concerned that you felt left out."

Laughter bubbled up and out. "Most gentlemen of my acquaintance use dancing when courting a lady. Once they secure the lady and marry, I believe most of them would be glad to never step on a ballroom floor ever again. More likely they are to be found in the game room most host and hostesses set up for just that reason. Along with bored husbands are single gentlemen hiding from the marriage mamas or overly forward debutantes hoping to snag a wealthy title."

"You make socializing sound dreadful. And that's not my experience with Wentworth and several of his friends. They appear to enjoy dancing with their wives." She paused, then smiled. "The more I think on it, the more I realize Wentworth, Myles, Bridgeton, and several others are the exception."

PENELOPE DIDN'T CARE if Newbury could never dance. She was being polite. Because truthfully, she didn't know what the extent of his injury to his knee was. For all she knew, he would heal in time and be swinging her around the dance floor in the future. As for Mr. Sinclair, she would hide in the retiring room for hours to avoid dancing... or waltzing... with him as she'd done at the masquerade ball. Her insides could not take any more guilt in being drawn to both cousins.

Would they ever exit the park? It felt as though she sat in the carriage for hours. Small talk wasn't her forte, so if she had to start discussing the weather she would scream. And wouldn't that cause quite the scandal.

Her mind wandered, not for the first time. For one moment she thought she sat next to Mr. Sinclair and had to remind herself it was Newbury. She had to keep reminding herself of his disfigurement. While sitting down driving the carriage, his perfect features facing her side, it was easy to forget who she was with. He resembled his cousin. They could be twins. Icy chills crawled up her spine. Perhaps Mr. Sinclair wasn't a cousin at all, but a by-blow from Newbury's father. That would explain the likeness between the two men.

"Mr. Sinclair needn't dance with me. I'm perfectly content to sit and watch." It wasn't a lie. Dancing caused her undo stress. When Mr. Sinclair held her close during that one waltz, even before she knew his true identity, it caused her heart to speed up and her body to tingle. Guilt bothered her as well. And after what happened on the veranda, they needed to keep their distance from each other.

A big sighed escaped her lips as she realized they'd pulled up in front of Wentworth Manor.

"Are you attending the opera this evening? Wentworth invited me to his box."

Her heart sank. She'd so been looking forward to her first opera. And it being *Don Giovanni* made it more exciting. Now she'd be sitting next to Newbury and tense the entire evening. "Yes."

"Splendid, I'm unfortunately unable to attend, but I accepted on behalf of Sinclair. I hope you enjoy the opera."

A footman stood waiting for Penelope who had been rendered speechless at the idea of spending the night in a dark box with Mr. Sinclair.

"Please forgive me for not exiting the carriage and bowing properly, my dear." He reached for her gloved hand.

Her eyes widened and her heart accelerated. He raised her hand up to his full lips, turned her wrist over, and placed his warm lips on her pressure point. She inhaled and held her breath, totally captivated. If she closed one eye, which she did not, and concentrated on the good half of his face, he turned into the most handsome man she'd ever seen. Handsome as Mr. Sinclair. "Until I see you again."

Once inside the house, Penelope entered the drawing room to find Emma sitting alone sipping tea and nibbling biscuits. "May I join you?"

"Yes. Please join me for refreshments as I recover from my day. I spent most of the afternoon with the children. We spent time running around the gardens and then playing in the nursery. I'm exhausted."

Perhaps Emma would be too exhausted to attend the opera that evening. Tired enough that Wentworth would cancel their plans.

"I see your mind working." Emma looked at her with compassion. "I'm not so tired I must stay home this evening. Besides, the more time you spend with the duke, the more comfortable you'll become with him." She poured tea for Penelope and handed her the delicate china cup and saucer. The S, for Seabrook, not visible from the bottom of the cup. But Penelope knew it was there. A reminder of who her family was.

"That's not it." She reached for a cube of sugar and plopped it in her tea. She enjoyed her tea extra sweet. "When he dropped me off, just now, he said he wouldn't be attending this evening and his cousin, would be taking his place. I don't understand why? Besides taking a drive in the park, do you think he doesn't want to be seen out in public with me again so soon?"

More compassion from Emma and for the first time Penelope realized how young she was. Because she was married to Wentworth and had two children, she forgot Emma was only one and twenty. "That is not why he's not attending the opera. Since Wentworth only extended the invitation yesterday, perhaps he has another engagement?"

Thinking about that, Penelope still wasn't convinced. It felt as though he were throwing Mr. Sinclair and her together. The question was why? "I tried to explain he need not always send his cousin in his place. But he didn't seem to take my words under advisement. Also, after the other night I don't trust Mr. Sinclair." Tingles danced up her spine, and she shivered. "He looks at me as though I'm his dessert. Like he wants to consume me. Most improper since I'm affianced to his cousin."

Emma gasped. "Indeed, most improper. If you don't mind me prying, how does the duke look at you?"

She had to fight not to laugh. Since the duke only had one eye, at times it was difficult to get a glimpse into his feelings. Except today, when he kissed her bare wrist, she witnessed the same hungry look in his one eye that she'd seen in Mr. Sinclair's two eyes. "Until today, I never noticed how he looked at me. Today he looked very much like his cousin. He looked at me with interest and want." Thinking about interest and want, she said, "I heard the duke has a mistress? Will he keep her after we wed?"

The feel of Emma's small, warm hand touching hers calmed her thoughts. "I don't know the answer to either of those questions, however, he appears to be an honorable man. Wentworth would hardly marry you off to a gentleman who wasn't. Perhaps after you wed, you can broach the subject of his mistress with him."

Now Penelope laughed. "I would never bring that up. How embarrassing. I can just imagine his reply. 'Yes, my dear, I have a mistress. Men have needs. Who is to fill those needs when a man is single? A mistress. And after a man weds, he has certain desires he can't ask his wife to perform for him. So, yes, Penelope, I have a mistress.'"

Emma joined her in laughter. "I can't imagine Newbury saying such nonsense. Which brings up something else. Do you need the night before your wedding speech about what happens between a husband and wife beneath the sheets? Bella, Amelia, and myself would be happy to enlighten you?"

Did she? Certainly not. She'd witnessed firsthand people procreating while living under the viscount's roof. Had nearly lost her virginity to the viscount. Servants partook in matters of the flesh often and not always in private. "I believe I'm well versed on that subject."

"I thought so." Emma frowned and looked thoughtful. "I'm sorry for what you and your mother went through. I believe if Thomas knew of you sooner, he would've sent for you and your mother. Once he found out my papa died and left me under his guardianship, he, along with Myles, traveled to Massachusetts to meet me. He waited until I finished Miss Beauregard's Finishing School before sailing back to England with me in tow. Between the travel time and the months in New Bedford running Hamilton Whaling Industries, nearly a year transpired. All because he felt obligated to honor my papa's wishes. Traveling to Northern England would have been nothing to Thomas."

"I'm grateful he came." Thinking back on her predicament, after her mother passed, had Penelope's insides knotting up tightly. She'd fled the viscount's house and found shelter with the local midwife, never expecting Wentworth would come for her or even respond to her missive. To her shock and dismay, he came with Mr. Stuart Spencer. Sebastian had traveled to her first but had been attacked by thieves and left for dead. Thankfully, his now wife, Teagan and her brother Lachlan Murray, had found him and nursed him back to health. Not a day went by that she didn't wonder how she got so lucky. How a duke could welcome into his family his dead father's natural born daughter. Dared anyone in polite society to contradict him when he introduced her as his sister. Even stood up for her with his own servants when they were less than respectful to her.

Those servants quickly found themselves with letters of recommendations, payment of wages owed, and an escort out the door. Tears pooled in her eyes at the length the Seabrook family had gone for her. Even the Dowager Duchess treated her kindly and with respect. If anyone had a right to treat her with contempt and distain the Dowager had.

"Perhaps you would like to rest before the evening meal and the opera. It will be a late evening again tonight," Emma suggested as she stood. "It's what I plan to do."

Sighing deeply, Penelope replied, "A rest sounds wonderful. Thank you, Your Grace."

"None of this, Your Grace, you must remember to call me Emma. At least when in the privacy of our home."

Penelope's maid helped her undress down to her chemise and tucked her into bed. "Please wake me in plenty of time to dress for this evening, Clarisse."

"Yes, milady."

Bone weary from the tug and pull of her emotions regarding Newbury and Mr. Sinclair, Penelope closed her eyes and was happy just to rest. Torn between her loyalty to her newly betrothed and her attraction to his cousin was wearing on her. On the ride through Hyde Park today, she found herself being pulled toward the duke. Surprisingly found herself interested and attracted to him. Of course, it helped that she sat on his good side. It seemed as if she rode with Mr. Sinclair. Was it possible they were brothers and not cousins? If that were true, why the secret? In fact, whenever in either of their company, instinct had her believing they both had secrets to hide. *Why? And what were they?*

Perhaps she would broach the subject with Mr. Sinclair this evening. He had said she could ask him anything pertaining to the duke. What she wanted to know was, who was he? Who was the real man behind the eye patch and scar? Sleep must have befallen her because before she knew it her maid was waking her up.

"I would like to wear the sky-blue gown this evening with the matching cloak."

"Yes, milady. That gown will look lovely with your eyes."

SITTING in the Seabrook family's private box at the opera with Wentworth, Emma, the Earl of Bridgeton, and his wife and her half-sister, Amelia, Penelope's eyes kept going from the empty seat beside her to Bella sitting across from them in the Northboroughs' private box. The lamps were still lit, but by how quickly the hall was filling up she knew the performance would start any minute. Where was Mr. Sinclair? She wanted to think she would be relieved if he never showed, but the truth was she would feel rejected. By both Newbury and Mr. Sinclair.

An attendant came into their box, snuffed the lamps and closed the curtains. Attendants worked diligently to darken the entire place and then the stage lit up and the opera began. Leaning forward, her heart pounding, Penelope became engrossed in the performers and singers on stage. Never had she seen such beautiful costumes, heard such lovely voices, or seen more gorgeous people. So transfixed by what transpired on stage, she never noticed when the seat beside her filled. Not until his gloved hand reached for hers and squeezed, shocking her. She pulled away and whispered, "You startled me."

He leaned close, his minty breath tickling her cheek. "Please accept my humble apologizes. I meant no harm."

If she didn't know Mr. Sinclair was going to take the duke's place, she would swear the duke himself sat beside her. But she knew better. There had been no clicking of his cane, which would have notified all occupants of the box the duke arrived. Possibly, even all occupants of the opera house. Which saddened her. No wonder Newbury stayed home. She may as well come to terms with that knowledge because in two months it would be her new reality as his duchess. She must become accustomed to people staring and whispering. As if they weren't already.

Before Mr. Sinclair spoke again, she felt the heat of his body leaning toward her and the warm air of his breath. "Have you attended the opera before?"

"No. And please be quiet." Since he joined her, the opera had lost her attention as all her nerve endings prickled with awareness of the man beside her. Shame on her. Since when was she a wicked person? Led by her emotions instead of her mind? She was duty and honor bound to Newbury. Why couldn't Mr. Sinclair move to the country and leave her be? Pain pierced her heart at the thought of him leaving even though it would be best for all parties.

The lights came on one by one and even though she'd never been to the theater; she knew it was intermission. Their lamps were lit, and the curtain thrown aside. She turned toward Mr. Sinclair and gasped.

"May I escort you downstairs for some refreshments?" Instead of Mr. Sinclair, the Duke of Newbury stood before her, offering his hand.

Her entire being paused, and she stammered, "But I...I thought you weren't attending?"

He chuckled. "I changed my mind, so I cancelled my prior engagement." The brow to his good eye rose in silent question. "Are you disappointed I'm here instead of my cousin?"

She recovered quickly. At least she believed she did. Her lips curved up into a smile as she placed her hand into his and stood. "Thank you. I'd love something to quench my parched throat."

His brow rose higher. "You didn't answer my query."

Her eyes moved around the box and was shocked to find it empty of anyone but the two of them. "Forgive me. No. I'm very pleased you decided to attend. I was surprised because I didn't hear you enter the box." She cleared her throat. "What I mean to say is…"

"I understand. I managed without my cane. Not an easy feat, but I didn't want to disturb anyone from enjoying the performance." One side of his mouth quirked up as he held up his cane with the metal lion's head. "I have need of it now with the crowd gathered about."

As they exited the box, Penelope and Newbury made their way awkwardly downstairs, being greeted by those members of the ton they were acquainted with. For her, the list was very short. For the duke, many bowed their heads and mumbled, "Your Grace." She got the impression he was well respected, but people didn't know how to handle his disfigurement so they almost ignored him or grumbled out his name or title. Uncomfortable pain reached her heart. How sad for Newbury. His peers should respect and honor him for his losses in defending the country against Bonaparte. His injuries weren't that hideous. In fact, the more time she spent with him, the more attractive he became. His injuries blending into the background. The black patch as Emma said made him resemble a pirate. As did the scar. Penelope could think of Newbury as a romantic pirate who sailed the seas in search of his bride. And didn't some pirates have a peg leg?

"Perhaps we should have stayed in the comfort and privacy of the box. It's a madhouse out here. Come this way." He led her to the right. "I see your family up ahead." They joined them and sipped champagne until the signal that the opera would continue in five minutes. It took that long for the six of them to settle back into their box. No sooner had they gotten comfortable, when the lights in their box and the theater seats below went out. The stage lights eliminated to reveal the second half of *Don Giovanni*.

The beautiful singing voices in Italian had Penelope leaning forward in her seat, mesmerized. Tears streamed down her cheeks as the performance unfolded.

SITTING BESIDE PENELOPE, Harry couldn't take his eyes off her. The box was shadowed in darkness, but he could make her out clearly because of his excellent sight. He spent enough time sneaking around in the blackness of night that his eyes adjusted well. His codename in the agency was Nighthawk because of his ultimate nighttime vision. And how he swept in for the arrest...or kill...depending on the circumstances.

Now, however, he enjoyed his better-than-average vision watching Penelope. Every emotion crossed her face as she concentrated solely on the performance on stage. Did she have any idea how the soft noises and subtle gasps she made had his insides coiling up tight with desire? Her eyes widening and lowering seductively. The tears streaming down her cheeks had his fingers itching to wipe them away and promise her anything never to cause her to cry again.

At one point, he frowned and took his eyes off her and

watched the stage. Even though it was known as a great opera, it didn't hold his attention. She called to him unknowingly, and he followed. Somehow, she turned him into a lovesick fool, and he'd yet to sample her. Her lips, her neck, her breasts…nothing. He'd sampled nothing, and yet she tied him in knots. Not something a gentleman wanted to admit. It was why he'd attended tonight as Harry and not Hugh.

He couldn't stomach the way she looked at him the other night as Hugh. He wanted. No, needed her to look at him—Harry—that way. With curiosity and unabashed lust. With a twinkle of mischief in her eyes as she waited on a kiss. A kiss he so desperately wanted to shower upon her lips, her neck, and down to swipe his tongue across the creamy swell of her breasts visible above her low neckline. A low moan escaped his lips before he realized it. If anyone heard, they politely didn't acknowledge it. Since he'd seen this opera once before he knew it would end momentarily, and he needed to turn his thoughts to something else besides the lovely woman who would become his wife.

As it appeared now, his breeches had a large bulge. It took ultimate restraint not to adjust himself and try to get it to behave. Fortunately for him, or unfortunately, no matter how you looked at it, his member wanted the lady beside him and it wanted her now.

The oil lamps were lit by workers at a frantic pace and the interior of the opera house came into clear focus, as well as their box. Time to make his exit before anyone noticed his extra snug breeches. Wentworth stood, stretched, and came to the front of the balcony. "Might as well sit for a time until the crowd thins out."

Voices around him discussed the opera, and he listened intently to Penelope, his eyes transfixed on her lovely face, as she retold her favorite parts with emotional abandon. It made him wonder how she would look and sound when he brought her pleasure in the bedroom. He also glimpsed, for the first time, how young she really was. She'd always appeared mature and wise beyond her seventeen years. No doubt due to her upbringing. Which had him wondering if she was even innocent? Not that it mattered to him.

"Your Grace." Penelope's questioning voice startled him from his thoughts. "It's time to leave."

Snapped to attention, he stood. "Bloody hell," he swore as he fumbled with his cane, which landed on the floor with a clatter. "Forgive me." He bent awkwardly at the waist, his leg out straight to the side and retrieved the cane. He held out his elbow to her and forced himself to soften his features, lest she run ahead in fright to her brother.

However, instead of fright at his clumsiness and sharpness, she looked concerned. "Take your time. We're in no hurry."

That solidified it. His heart physically melted and pooled at her delicate, slipper covered feet. The lady had a heart of gold. Why did she treat him with such kindness? Couldn't she see the man beneath? The man who struggled with demons that visited him on a regular basis and claimed to own his soul. A man who could kill without remorse.

"You appear to be lost in your thoughts again, Your Grace."

Once again he apologized. "We must hurry, or Wentworth will become worried."

She blushed. A sweet, innocent shade of pink. "My brother gave me permission to ride to Wentworth Manor with you since we are, after all, betrothed. He thought we may have things to discuss."

If Penelope said the sky was brown, he'd be less shocked at Wentworth's decision. Harry had sent a note, after their ride in the park, asking for permission to escort her home. Since he hadn't received a response, he'd taken it as a decline.

Either Wentworth had changed his mind or planned to allow him this privacy to occur all along.

"Please extend my gratitude to him. When I didn't get a response to my letter, I took it as a decline."

Her head snapped his way and her eyes widened as they exited the opera house. "I hadn't realized the request came from you. I thought my brother was being kind."

"He is being kind." Harry signaled his driver with his cane. "Here we are." The driver hopped down from his perch, opened the door to the grand carriage, and lowered the steps. Harry assisted Penelope inside the coach, then climbed in and sat down beside her on the cushioned seat facing forward. A chilly rain had settled over London, so he reached on the opposite bench and covered her lap with a blanket. He ignored the sudden ache in his knee and shoulder because of bullet wounds.

"Thank you," she said hesitantly. Shy? Was she being shy around him? He didn't blame her. If she knew what he wanted to do with her in the carriage's privacy, beneath the cover of darkness, she should be shy and nervous. Too bad he wouldn't act on his desires. Except?

He slid toward her on the bench until they touched from shoulder, to hip, to thigh, to knee, and Harry swallowed down a groan of pleasure to finally be pressed up against her lovely figure. "I wanted some privacy with you this evening to discuss if there is anything you want to know about me to ease your anxiety about our upcoming nuptials."

A brief gasp escaped her lips. Perhaps he was being too forward.

"I...I." Penelope was at a loss for words. There was much she wanted to know about the gentleman sitting beside her. So close she could hardly breathe. And when she did, his sandal-wood cologne tickled her nose in a pleasant way. She'd noticed that about him the first time they met, that he smelled divine. "We have the rest of our lives to get to know one another. I can wait for my questions."

Her hands toyed with the satin reticle on her lap. He reached over with his bare hands, having removed his gloves when they entered the coach, and took one of hers in his hand. Before she realized what he had in mind, he gently tugged on her white glove at each fingertip, sending waves of tingles from the tips of her fingers straight up her arm. For such large hands, they were surprisingly tender as her glove vanished. He brought her newly naked hand up to his lips and placed warm kisses on each digit. Which had her trans-fixed. Her eyes never looked away from his one blue eye, which had darkened to near ebony. Breathing became labo-rious as her heart pounded inside her chest. A slow burn settled inside her stomach, and she licked her dry lips. A moan escaped his lips, sending sultry air blowing across her wet fingers, and she nearly groaned as well. What was happening to her? Was this what desire felt like? Her eyelids suddenly felt heavy, she had to fight to keep them open. And she wanted Newbury to do something to relieve the pressure down below.

He turned her hand over, palm up, and delicately pushed her sleeve up. Every scrape of fabric sent tingles across her over-sensitive skin. Before she knew what he planned to do his tongue swirled around the inside of her wrist causing her to, not moan, but sigh deeply. Mortified at her reaction to him she tugged her hand free, but he refused to let it go.

"Please don't deny me this minor pleasure of touching you. It will have to hold me over until our wedding night."

Did he plan on touching her elsewhere? The answer came as he turned on the bench and cradled her face in his large hands, causing her to close her eyes. When they fluttered open, she stared at his cravat, afraid at what she may glimpse in his eye.

"Look at me."

She did. In the muted darkness with only one lantern lit inside the carriage, his scar blended in and the black patch made him appear dangerously handsome. It wasn't the first time she found him handsome. Right this moment he stole the very breath in her lungs, and she hoped he kissed her. Surely that was his plan...

Desire shone in his eye and he dipped his head, taking her lips with his. They were soft, gentle, barely grazing her lips which tingled at the delicate touch. It didn't take long for things to change. His body tensed, he swore against her lips, then put pressure on her mouth until she gasped, parting her lips. His tongue swept inside, his arms went around her back and pulled her tight against him.

Instinct had her arms curling around his neck and she rubbed her breasts against his hard chest, trying to satisfy the tingling in her nipples. The angle of his head changed, and he deepened the kiss. His tongue thrust in and out of her mouth, and she tried to mimic him until they tangled together and she wondered if she'd done something wrong when he growled. His hand moved to her front, and she held her breath as he undid the frog clasps to her cloak and pushed it off her shoulders. The cool night air kissed her bare skin. Before she could comprehend that it chilled her, his warm lips traveled down her neck and across the swell of her partially exposed breasts causing a sudden inferno that had her wanting to tear off her clothes and be free.

"You are so beautiful, my dear." Teeth lightly scraped across the tops of her breasts. Breasts that begged to be free of their confinement.

So lost in her emotions and lust, she never realized

Newbury had popped free her heavy breasts until his tongue laved one bare nipple. "Oh my," she breathed as she arched her back in supplication.

He responded by sucking her nipple deep into his mouth while one of his hands kneaded her other breast. She gasped as his other hand slid up her leg, leaving a wake of goose bumps behind. Up over her calf. Over her knee, up the inside of her thigh. *When had I parted my legs?* Until he cupped her there. The slit in her pantaloons giving her no protection from his questing fingers as they sought out her womanhood.

To her mortification she moaned, her thighs parted wider, and her hips pushed into his hand repeatedly. What must he be thinking? That he was marrying a wanton? "Mmmmm." She moaned again, unable to stop her body's betrayal. Her body's need for something as he pushed a finger inside her, nearly sending her off the bench. "Hugh?" It was the first time she used his Christian name. It felt right on her tongue.

Time paused. The fog in her brain refused to relent until she heard the rustling of her clothing being put to right.

A hand gripped her chin painfully and forced her face up. "Look at me," Newbury demanded.

Her eyes popped open, and she glimpsed hurt, anger, and disappointment in his one eye. Why? What had she done wrong?

"When I claim you on our wedding night," he sneered, his voice deep and angry, "try to remember my name."

He banged on the front wall of the carriage and seconds later the driver opened the door and assisted with her descent.

"Please see the lady safely inside."

Standing in the large welcoming foyer of Wentworth Manor, Penelope felt anything but welcome. What happened just now inside the carriage? Had she done something wrong? Why had he treated her poorly at the end? Hiking up her skirts, she hurried up the stairs to her room. Waved her maid away mumbling, "I can undress myself." Instead of undressing she unclasped her cloak, let it fall silently to the floor, and fell onto the bed on her stomach. Tears leaked from her eyes, wetting the coverlet, so she rolled over onto her back, hugged herself, and cried even more. Her mind traveled back to the moment Newbury became angry with her. Had she said or done something? A loud gasp escaped her lips, and she shot up. "Oh my God, I called him Hugh."

HARRY STOMPED AROUND THE LIBRARY, drinking straight from a bottle of whiskey, swearing loudly at himself for the fool he was. Edmond entered the room, took the bottle from his hands, and placed it on the credenza.

"What has you in such a foul mood?"

"The little twit called me Hugh," he spat out as he swayed toward a chair and crumpled down in it. It was either that or fall flat onto the floor. On his face. He was smashed.

"She did, did she now?"

"I may not be able to see straight, but I can tell from your voice you're finding this amusing. And I don't want to hear, 'I warned you.'"

"Well...your words not mine." Edmond went to the sideboard and helped himself to a glass of fine brandy the Duke of Wentworth sent to Harry. "Care to share just what was transpiring when Lady Penelope referred to you as Hugh?"

He swayed forward and almost tumbled out of the chair. "No. I don't. Suffice it to say, she'll never make the mistake again."

"Once you are wed and divulge your secret, I dare say not."

The room wouldn't stop moving. He closed his eyes, opened his eyes, and still the walls moved in a circular motion as did Edmond. "Sit the bloody hell down, you're making me dizzy."

Snorting, Edmond did as he was told. "You do realize, there's a possibility Lady Penelope will never speak to you again when she finds out? She will think you made a fool of her. Not the best way to start a marriage."

Harry swung his head Edmond's way, then cringed. He loathed when he drank to excess. He would hate himself even more in the morning when he was puking his guts out. His stomach rolled—or sooner. "I know. But how else am I s-s-s-supposed to handle this dilemma?"

"Confide in her now and put the poor girl out of her misery in thinking she's marrying a one-eyed, scarred gimp."

That remark brought laughter to Harry's lips. Put the way Edmond said it sounded either horrifying or humorous. Indeed, only he and those who knew would find it humorous. Others, such as Penelope, would find being settled with him for life horrifying. Damn. He had some ruminating to do.

THE FOLLOWING DAY, with a head twice its size, a nagging headache, and a stomach that refused to keep anything down, Harry sent for Mr. Smythe. The Runner had had plenty of time to think about the job offer and to investigate Harry and the position he held within the War Office. Promptly at half eleven, he was announced. Harry stood, leaning on the desk, playing the part of the cripple. He

THE SPY AND HIS LADY LOVE

gestured to a chair opposite his mahogany desk. "Please have a seat."

Smythe bowed. "Thank you, Your Grace." And waited until Harry sat.

"May I offer you some brandy or whiskey?"

"No, thank you. If you don't mind, I'd like to get down to business."

"Certainly." The Runner seemed almost agitated with him. Had he uncovered his secret and took offense? "Have you come to a conclusion about the offer?"

Harry wasn't surprised Smythe's face gave nothing about his decision away. He was, after all, the best Runner in London to date. Had to keep his emotions blank. Otherwise his enemies would know his thoughts and he would be dead. One of the reasons he was so valuable to the Crown.

"I've thought long and hard about the offer. And I must decline."

Sitting back in his seat, Harry eyed Smythe with a raised brow in his one uncovered eye. "You do realize I'm merely the messenger for the Regent? He is the one who recommended you for the position. If I were you, I would think wisely about changing your answer."

Smythe sat up straighter and leaned forward just a tad in the chair. The only sign he gave of unease. "I did not understand."

"Perhaps, at our first meeting, I neglected to mention it." Harry paused and if he looked deep enough into the man's eyes, he could see the wheels in motion as he rethought his decision. "Is there anything I can do to persuade you to change your mind?" Harry purposely didn't disclose that little tidbit of information about the prince. Most men would jump at the opportunity when the prince's name was mentioned. Which was why it never was. Except now. He wanted the man on his team. And truthfully would do anything to get him. When it came to his position, Harry was ruthless. If only he could be more ruthless in his personal life. A little pain settled inside his chest. He would not think about her now.

"Why did you lie to me?"

"Quite bold to accuse a duke and a member of the War Office of lying. In what way did I do so?"

"In pretending to be injured. As in being two people, The Duke of Newbury and Mr. Hugh Sinclair, your distant cousin."

"So you are as good as they say." Newbury removed the patch from his eye and used his handkerchief to remove as much of the make-up that he could which created his scar. He'd not worn the brace on his knee, which truth be told, he needed sometimes from an actual injury. Smythe didn't so much as twitch at the revelation. "Forgive me for deceiving you. I stay alive because of my disguises. As the crippled duke, I'm ignored at most society functions and for some reason people think I'm daft in the head as well. They look past me and divulge secrets and espionage. Especially at my clubs. Many members at Whites' or Brooks', once in their cups, spill all sorts of secrets."

"If I take the position, why would anyone spill secrets to a former Runner against the Crown."

"As I explained at our first meeting, we will create a scandal having you demoted. Which in turn you will quit and swear vengeance on the Crown. It will only be a matter of time before the unsavory contact you with offers of allegiance to the under belly of England. Which no doubt will bring forth those loyal to France."

"What if you are wrong?"

Harry shrugged one shoulder. Pretending calm when he was anything but. "Then we will come up with another plan."

"May I tell my wife?"

"Since I find myself in a precarious situation with my upcoming marriage and dealing with two identities, one which will be hard to remain hidden in the bedchamber, I will allow it."

For the first time the Runner let his emotions slip. He sighed and relaxed against the back of the chair. "Then my answer is yes. If you don't mind, I'll take that brandy now, Your Grace."

Standing, Newbury poured both of them a generous portion. Smythe downed half his glass, then sipped the rest. "Thank you. The only time I've tasted brandy this good was from Wentworth."

"Then you can thank him as he sent me a case." Harry didn't dare take a sip; the smell alone had his stomach rolling. He placed the glass untouched on his desk. "Please, only call me by my title when we encounter each other out in society. Otherwise, Harry will do. Unless I'm dressed as Hugh. Then Hugh, please. My code name within the War Office is Nighthawk. I believe Gunslinger is quite apt for you. Any objections?"

"None at all."

"Good." Now that business was concluded, Harry had some personal questions for Smythe.

"You do know I'm marrying Wentworth's sister, Penelope, in just a little over a fortnight?"

"Yes. I do. We have been invited."

"Good. I've a major dilemma, and since you are in the inner circle of friends with the Seabrooks, I've a personal question to ask of you."

Smythe's hand tightened on the glass as he took a sip of the amber liquid. The only telltale sign he was uncomfortable. "I'll answer depending on the question? I won't divulge anything to do with the times they have hired me."

"Not asking you to. It has to do with Lady Penelope and

the fact she's marrying one person who has two personas." He paused and dared a sip of his drink. "I'm torn between telling her before the wedding or afterwards."

"Definitely a delicate issue. Lady Penelope is a strong woman. If you want a meek and dutiful wife, you have chosen quite the opposite."

"Exactly why I have chosen her. I never expected to inherit the dukedom. I grew up on a farm, planned to stay in the army for life. She comes from rather less than stellar beginnings, not that I hold that against her, in fact, it works to my advantage. I rather like the idea of marrying into the Seabrook family and within it their circle of close friends. Never would've happened if she'd been legitimate. Wentworth would have found someone more suitable for a gently bred girl. However, I do not want to anger Wentworth or my soon-to-be-wife."

"I'm afraid I'm at a loss for advice."

Harry stood, concluding the meeting. "I was testing you. Welcome to the War Office. After my wedding, the events of your demotion will take place. For the time being I will create rumors of you taking bribes and payouts down in St. Giles. No one will doubt it since that's where you come from and lived until recently. Please inform your wife soon. I don't want to cause undo problems within your marriage. As for informing her brother, Spencer, I will think on it."

Once alone, Harry's thoughts turned to Penelope and the intimacy they'd shared the night of the opera, making him think it was time to send her a message.

## CHAPTER 6

"Have you received any correspondences from the Duke of Newbury?" Penelope asked as she entered Thomas's study one afternoon only two weeks' time from the nuptials. After the night at the opera when she called him Hugh, the only communication was a hot house delivery of four dozen blood red roses with a card in large letters signed, H A R R Y, underlined three times. She'd not found it humorous and had taken offense.

If she'd insulted him, he never should have sent Mr. Sinclair in his place to dance and pay attention to her. The fault lay completely on him. Served him right if she'd fallen for his cousin. Except, that wasn't true. She felt attraction to Mr. Sinclair, but Harry intrigued her, made her want to know everything about him. And his kisses...she wanted more."

"What has you blushing?"

Good Lord, she forgot she was in Thomas's study. "Nothing. Have you heard from His Grace?"

"Yes. Just his morning. He said he'll arrive at Stoney Cross Manor two days before the wedding." He leaned forward, elbows on the desk, his chin leaning on his hands. "Did I make a mistake by allowing him to escort you home from the opera? Did something happen in the carriage? We've not heard from him or seen him or his cousin in over a month?"

Indeed, something did happen. In the heat of passion, she whispered the name of Hugh. Embarrassed beyond words, she could not admit such things to her brother. "Nothing that I know of. Perhaps he has taken ill?"

"Perhaps." Thomas looked at her with intense blue eyes, nearly the same color as hers, seeking her secrets. And she fought to remain still.

"If you'll excuse me, Thomas, I think I will spend time with my nephews in the nursery."

He chuckled. "You best change into a dress you don't mind ruining."

Her heart lighter than when she entered his study, she made her way up two flights of stairs to the third floor and the nursery where she could hear laughter and squeals coming from inside. Leaning against the door jam, her heart warmed at the sight of the two boys sitting on the floor, climbing all over Emma who wore wide puffy trousers.

"I dare say, Your Grace, no one would recognize you in your attire." Emma burst out laughing as the two mischievous boys tickled her tummy. Then she rolled them over and did the same thing until their laughter could, no doubt, be heard two floors down. Such a happy house they all lived in. Penelope's breath tangled up inside her lungs. She won't live in a happy house much longer.

They decided to take the boys out in the gardens and let them run off some of their endless energy before naptime. After their nurse tucked the boys into bed, both Emma and Penelope yawned. "I could use a nap myself," Emma said as they descended the stairs. "Since it's almost teatime, I believe I'll change and hope the tea revives me."

"Me as well," Penelope said as she entered her bedchamber and rang for her maid. Revitalized and dressed in a lovely pale blue frock, she made her way down the stairs to the drawing room. Her feet came to a crashing stop just inside the doorway when she saw Newbury sitting in a chair, sipping tea, and animatedly conversing with Emma and Wentworth who sat opposite him on the pink velvet settee.

She must have gasped or made some sort of noise because suddenly three sets of eyes settled on her face. Putting her shock aside at finding the duke here, she forced a smile and made her way forward to join them. She curtsied before Newbury. "Your Grace, what a lovely surprise to see you." As he reached for his cane, she waved him off. "Please stay seated." After taking the chair beside his she reached for the tea cup Emma prepared for her and took a sip, hoping Newbury didn't notice how her hand shook, causing the cup to clank against the saucer.

"We were just discussing the weather," Thomas said as he cleared his throat after taking a swallow of tea. "How can anyone drink this dreadful stuff without sweetener." He reached forward and plucked two sugar cubes from a bowl and dropped them into his tea with a loud plop.

Both Emma and Penelope laughed at Thomas, making Emma explain, "My husband tries to drink his tea with cream and no sugar but caves to adding two cubes. Amesbury and Myles have teased him relentlessly about not drinking tea like a man and saying only women add sugar. It is a sore subject and one that brings joy to those who watch him struggle with it."

"Yes, well, I prefer coffee to tea any time of the day," Newbury said as he placed his empty china cup and saucer on the table and picked up a biscuit.

"I agree," Thomas said."

"Your Grace," Penelope began, did you come to discuss plans for our upcoming wedding?"

"Yes, I wanted to talk with you about our wedding day." He paused and looked at her brother. "I was hoping, with your permission, Wentworth, to have a few moments alone with my intended to discuss our honeymoon."

No sooner had the words left Newbury's mouth than both Emma and Thomas stood and excused themselves from the room. Emma left the door to the room open barely an inch. Basically leaving the duke and her completely alone and with all the privacy they could want. *Do I want to be in a private room with the duke? Not after what happened in the coach the night we attended the opera.*

Before Penelope could come up with something to say, Newbury stood and made his way to look out a large picture window that overlooked the formal gardens out back. His cane stayed beside his chair and he walked, taking a step with his good leg and swinging his bad leg forward. Over and over until he reached the window. It was painfully awkward to watch him struggle. Although it didn't seem to bother him and he made surprisingly quick progress.

"Would you mind joining me."

It was presented as a statement, not a question. After placing her half-eaten biscuit on her plate, she rose and softly walked across the oriental rug to stand beside the duke. As her pulse soared and her palms dampened she tried to calm herself by inhaling and exhaling slow and steady.

"I beg forgiveness for my behavior the night we attended the opera," Newbury said as he stared out the window as though something interesting held his attention. "I should have escorted you to the door. It was quite rude of me. There is no excuse for my poor judgment."

She opened her mouth to speak several times before she could come up with something to say besides thank you.

"There is no need to apologize. You did not hurt my feelings or insult me with your decision to stay inside the coach. I presumed your leg was bothering you. Besides, I believe, correct me if I'm wrong, that as a betrothed couple, are we not allowed to relax on certain formalities when not in public. And the same when we are finally wed." From what she had observed from her married family members, they relaxed all formality when in the privacy of their homes and surrounded by family and close friends. She certainly hoped he didn't want all the bowing, curtsying, and formality to exist between them when in the privacy of their home.

"Yes. But that night…" He paused, turned to look at her, and she gasped at the intensity in his deep blue eye and the thoughtful frown on his face. "I thought we made progress toward the intimacy we will share as husband and wife. I should have respected you and seen you properly inside your residence."

Before she could stop herself she blurted out, "And I should not have called you Hugh." She slapped her hand over her mouth and wished she could crawl beneath the carpet and hide forever. As she waited for him to say something… anything, heat scorched her cheeks, her body trembled, and tears pooled in her eyes. Whether from anger at herself, from shame, or embarrassment. Most definitely all three. What really bothered her was the pain she briefly witnessed before he buried his emotions to a blank look and stare. Time stood still as she waited and waited.

Finally, one side of his mouth quirked up into a smile and his eye softened as well as the rest of his features. She swore she could see the tension in his body ease as well. "If you forgive me for my rudeness, I'll forgive you for calling out my cousin's name…in the throes of passion."

He had to use the word passion? "I forgive you. My referring to you as someone else's name will never happen again."

Pain radiated inside her at her mortification. Once she and Newbury were married, seeing Mr. Sinclair on a regular basis would be awkward. Perhaps Mr. Sinclair would find other lodgings. Wouldn't bachelor quarters be more to his liking? She could only hope.

The three of them living in the same house would only cause unnecessary tension.

"Thank you for your forgiveness. And I will pretend you never referred to me as another, provided it doesn't happen again."

"It won't." She prayed with all her heart she told the truth.

"Then." He moved close to her, his warm hands gently cupping her cheeks, causing her to inhale as she waited for his lips to touch hers. When they did, she closed her eyes, wrapped her arms around his neck and leaned into him. The kiss, as before, started out gentle and teasing. He licked across her lips, silently asking permission to enter. Her lips parted and he thrust his tongue inside her mouth and she twirled her tongue around with his. Need pooled inside her belly, she moaned and pressed her breasts against his hard chest. Seeking to repeat the feelings he gave her in the coach and wanting to touch him, she moved her hands to his face and just as her fingertips grazed his skin his fingers curled around her wrists and pulled them away. He stepped back out of reach. Oh God, she'd forgotten about his face and murmured, "I'm sorry."

They stood several feet apart, both breathing heavily, and she noticed his features were flush as she knew hers to be as well. What shocked her was he looked as moved by the kiss as she was.

"No need to apologize. I should've told you I don't like my face touched."

"I'll remember for…next time."

"Thank you."

The air between them thickened with tension, and she didn't know how to change it. "Did you really want to discuss our honeymoon with me?"

~

HE'D FORGOTTEN ALL about that. "Yes. Unfortunately, due to my work schedule, we'll have to postpone our honeymoon until a later date. I promise I will take you on a trip to the continent in the very near future."

The kiss they shared had his body strung up tighter than a violin, and just now his heart slowed down to a normal beat. He needed to be very careful with her. He'd almost let her touch his face. Been so lost in their kiss, he'd almost missed her hands moving. Until he divulged his secret, he had to be more careful. It didn't help that he craved her touch everywhere on his body including his face. Hopefully, his actions just now didn't frighten her away from touching him once they wed. When he'd gripped her wrists and pulled away, he'd seen the shock register on her face. And a little bit of pain as he'd gripped her wrists tightly in his panic.

"I believe you are attending a musical this evening at the home of Mr. and Mrs. Cavanaugh. I wish I could attend, but alas I cannot. My cousin will be in attendance and will seek you out." He bowed. "Good day, Lady Penelope."

In his haste to leave, he almost forgot his cane. Good thing he wore his brace, otherwise he would have walked with only the slightest limp, or none at all, giving himself away.

~

THE RIDE to the musical seemed to take forever as Penelope looked out the window into the darkness beyond, wondering

85

what was holding them up. Not long after they approached a coach with a broken wheel, Wentworth signaled the driver to pull over and see if they were in need of assistance.

How fortunate or unfortunate for her that it was Mr. Sinclair's carriage with the broken wheel. Wentworth invited him to travel with them when he realized they were both attending the Cavanaugh's musical. Wentworth climbed in the carriage first and took his seat beside Emma. "Mr. Sinclair is joining us since he's having transportation issues. You remember my wife, the duchess, and my sister, Lady Penelope?"

Mr. Sinclair took the seat beside her and nodded his head first to Emma and then to her. "Yes. It's a pleasure to see both of you again. And I must thank you for rescuing me. Dreadful thing when a carriage breaks down."

"We are happy to give you a ride," Emma said with a gracious smile.

"I understand, after speaking to Newbury, that plans for the wedding are coming along nicely," Mr. Sinclair said.

Wentworth replied, "Yes. It was a pleasant surprise when he dropped by for tea this afternoon."

"Yes. He told me. Let me say how sorry I am that I'll be away taking care of business when the wedding takes place." Mr. Sinclair pivoted in his seat and looked right at Penelope, and she shivered.

Why did his eyes have the same effect on her as the duke's? Was it because their color and their looks were so similar? That looking into Mr. Sinclair's eyes was like looking into the duke's? And their features. So familiar? The reasoning did not matter, what mattered was how her body responded, making her confused. How could she be in Newbury's arms this afternoon, kissing him and willing to give herself to him. Then wanting the same with his cousin. Could she be losing her mind?

"I'm sorry. His Grace must be disappointed as you are his only living relative," Penelope said as she dropped her eyes to her lap to hide her disappointment.

"He understands completely."

Thank goodness they arrived because Penelope needed fresh air. The cologne Mr. Sinclair wore was the same as Newbury, making her wonder why they both preferred the same scent of sandalwood. Perhaps Mr. Sinclair had no cologne of his own and borrowed from Newbury. No matter the reasoning, it unsettled her to have them both smelling the same.

Penelope sat in the third row between Emma and Mr. Sinclair. Wentworth sat on Emma's other side. *Really?* she huffed. Wasn't it bad enough they'd given the man a ride, did he have to insinuate himself into their party and take the seat beside her? She knew she was being unkind, but couldn't help herself.

"I don't understand why these poor girls have to perform." Mr. Sinclair leaned close to Penelope, and the warmth from his body melted into hers. "Two of them are good, but the poor youngest one hasn't had time to perfect her voice or violin. If their parents are seeking husbands for them, I wish them well." He paused. "Although the eldest daughter is quite fetching. I would consider her myself if I was in the market for a wife."

Quickly, she covered her mouth before an unladylike noise escaped and made its way to all the ears in the room. Mr. Sinclair thought highly of himself. What made him think Mr. and Mrs. Cavanaugh would even consider him for one of their daughters? "I believe they are seeking titles. And unless I'm mistaken, you do not possess one."

He leaned closer, and his minty breath wafted across her cheek. "If Newbury dies, who do you think takes over the title?"

Once again, she covered her mouth to stifle her rude noises. "Let's pray that never comes to fruition, and he has many heirs."

"You do realize those heirs will be yours as well."

The insufferable man. "Please be quiet, I'd like to enjoy the music."

"Forgive me for disturbing you."

After the Cavanaugh girls' performance ended they spread out into the ballroom for refreshments. Mr. Sinclair followed them as though he belonged in their party. It was most perturbing. How was she to relax and remember society's rules of etiquette if she was constantly on edge from being near his person. She rather hated the guilty emotions he welded up inside her. Guilt for being attracted to both him and Newbury. Why did the cousins have to resemble each other in looks and mannerisms?

"You seem annoyed with Mr. Sinclair this evening?" Emma whispered as Wentworth and Mr. Sinclair moved away to speak with several other gentlemen in attendance.

*Am I that obvious?* "For some reason he annoys me. Perhaps because he looks so much like Newbury I find it unsettling. It makes me wish the roles were reversed and Mr. Sinclair was damaged and Newbury perfect." She gasped and slapped her mouth, her eyes darting nervously around them. "I'm a horrible person. How will I ever be able to be a duchess? I can't believe the prince is even allowing such a match. There are very few dukes, and one shouldn't be wedding a bastard."

"Hush, Penelope," Emma scolded as she looked around. Then let out a breath. "Thank goodness I don't think anyone heard you. You mustn't call yourself that. Wentworth has worked hard to elevate you up in society. He betrothed you to a duke. And not just any duke. The Newbury Dukedom is one of the oldest and wealthiest." Emma gasped. "Oh dear, I sound like an uptight English aristocrat. Not the American I was born."

"Indeed, you do. As to the Newbury Dukedom. Yes. So I've been told it's one of the oldest and wealthiest. Wentworth should not have bothered. I would have been perfectly happy marrying a country squire." She told the truth. She would much prefer to live in the country out of the eyes and ears of the ton. What if she embarrassed the duke once they wed? There was still much she needed to learn about the aristocracy. Newbury was a duke. Would they be expected to host balls and the Prince Regent? From what she'd heard, Newbury was close friends with the man.

Emma smiled beautifully. "Here are our men. We must take our leave."

"Our men? Surely you realize Mr. Sinclair is not my man."

Emma's cheeks pinked. "Yes. That isn't what I meant."

Penelope found herself sharing the cushioned bench with Mr. Sinclair…again as he shared their carriage…again. Once or twice his leg brushed up against hers. Whether from accident or on purpose, she couldn't tell. And she refused to acknowledge the heat burning her skin through her skirts from his muscular leg. His hand also brushed against her thigh. The man was a rakehell, a ne'er-do-well, and didn't belong anywhere near her in a dark conveyance when her chaperons had their eyes closed across from her.

"Are you looking forward to your wedding?" his voice asked in a whisper, very close to her ear.

"Why yes, Mr. Sinclair, I am."

"Liar." His breath heated her earlobe, and she fought the urge to squirm on the seat. This attraction had to stop. Being anywhere near him had to stop. How was she to be an exemplary wife to Newbury when she desired his cousin? And she desired Newbury. What was wrong with her? She'd experienced no physical or emotional attraction to any man before. Why now? And why two different men?"

"You seem lost in thought. Care to share? You know I will keep your secrets."

His words brought a curse to her lips.

"Easy there, Lady Penelope, if you say such things in public, people will bring up your less than stellar entrance into this world."

Before she realized what she was about to do, she smacked him in the arm with her reticle. Too bad it wasn't full of rocks and would cause actual damage. "How could you..."

The noise woke up Wentworth and Emma. "What was that noise?" Wentworth asked as he pulled aside the curtain and peered out the window.

"Sounded like the driver ran over something," Mr. Sinclair replied.

"Yes, well. If it was anything to be concerned about, we would be stopping."

"We are Your Grace," Mr. Sinclair said with a grin. "We have arrived at Newbury House."

The driver opened the door and let down the stairs.

Once outside he bowed. "Thank you for your hospitality this evening. Duke, Duchess, Lady Penelope."

"He appears to be an affable gentleman," Wentworth said as the carriage got underway. "I would consider him marrying into the family if I had any more sisters to marry off." His laughter rang throughout the coach. "Thank goodness I don't."

Penelope and Emma laughed along with him. Yes. Thank goodness she was the last to marry off. She didn't want to contemplate Mr. Sinclair marrying into the Seabrook family. It was bad enough she was marrying into his.

HARRY DISLIKED WALKING in the front door. One never knew who might be watching his home. But he didn't want Wentworth to think something strange if he went around back. He handed his greatcoat, hat, and gloves to his doorman and was told his valet awaited him in his room. As he ascended the stairs, he wondered why Edmond needed to see him immediately upon his return.

"There you are," Edmond said as he handed Harry a glass of whiskey. "You will need this."

Harry cocked a brow. "Why may I ask?"

"Kincaid and James were murdered in Kincaid's home earlier this evening. Their throats slit."

After downing his whiskey, Newbury paced the sitting room off his bedchamber. His heart ached and instantly his entire body tensed up painfully tight. "They were made?"

"Yes," Edmond answered.

Visions of his dead colleagues sent fear running through his veins for the safety of all the spies within the War Office. Which also included several women. He would never forgive himself for attending a musical, trying to get to know his intended better, instead of hunting down the enemy. Letting the enemy snuff out the lives of honorable men. One which had a wife and two small children. Pausing, he looked down at his hand, still holding the empty glass. He raised his arm and threw it at the fireplace with a crash.

Too bad the satisfaction of destroying something lasted only moments. Stopping at the small desk he kept in his sitting room, he scribbled off a message to Smythe and handed it to Edmond. "Deliver this right away and don't leave without him."

An hour later Harry had nearly worn a path in the Aubusson carpet in the library. He scribbled off several more messages and had them delivered. He waited anxiously to hear from Prinny.

Where the bloody hell were Edmond and Smythe? He was reaching here, but he hoped the Runner had some information on the deaths? No sooner had the thoughts entered his mind than the two gentlemen walked into the library.

"Please sit," Harry said as he stood in front of the hearth, enjoying the heat from the flames against his chilled body. Not just chilled, numb, shock, whatever it was had his insides frozen.

"Thank you for coming at such an ungodly hour. Two of the War Office's top spies were murdered. Throats slit."

"Yes. I know. I sent a Runner over with the Guard Arms to investigate. At the time I figured it was a theft gone bad. Then when my man returned and reported to me that uniforms from the Secretary of War's Office arrived and made everyone leave I figured they were not your average men." Smythe wore rumpled clothing and looked exhausted, complete with dark circles beneath his eye and stress lines bracketing his mouth. "I'd only just crawled into bed when your man here arrived." He rubbed the stubble on his jaw. "Bloody long night and only getting longer."

"Have you heard any rumors about Kincaid and James? I know you have connections in the underbelly of London, St. Giles, and the rockeries. Your own network of spies feeding you information. And possibly a Runner or two who are crooked."

"We've had our share of crooked Runners. Caught one last year, and he's comfortably rotting in Newgate. Have you considered a double spy has infiltrated your organization? One with the task of murdering all members of the War Office? But I also must add that it is widely known that Newbury in full disguise, works for the War Office. Why has no one tried to kill you?"

"Yes, it is known, or rumored, that I work for the War Office as a delegate. Not as a spy. Most think I'm harmless and have no proper authority. Which is what we want people to think. Meanwhile, have you any thoughts about Baron Littleton. We've been investigating him since the war ended. Unfortunately, all we have on him is hearsay. We have no proof of his crimes against the Crown. But he has been our prime focus of late. One reason I recruited you. I believe you will pique his interest once you're fired from your present job and insinuated back into the underbelly of London."

Smythe frowned. "I thought I would be demoted, then quit."

Harry ran his hands through his hair. "Changed my mind. Firing you would get you working undercover faster. And with these two murders, it's something we need. The sooner I have you onboard the better."

"I'm still worried about my wife and her family."

"I know. I'm still working out the logistics."

"So. Are we still waiting until after your wedding to fire me?" Smythe said with a knowing grin.

"No. They will fire you tomorrow on suspicion of murder."

"Whose?" Shaking his head, he added, "Never mind. I can guess. It's the perfect setup."

"Indeed." Harry paused as something else bothered him. "I may have to postpone my wedding to Lady Penelope. I can't possibly leave for several days when my peoples' lives are in peril. Not to mention, I'd rather not bring her into this mess and put her life in danger as well."

Smythe visibly tensed. "Perhaps Mary should spend time with her family. If I don't send her away, once I'm fired, Spencer will, no doubt, take her home and away from me."

"I'm sorry to put you in this situation."

"It's something I agreed to. I'll deal with the repercussions."

"Edmond, is there anything you want to add?"

"Starting tomorrow we work in pairs. A lot of good it did for Kincaid and James, but I advise you should strictly enforce the pair issue."

"Superb idea. I will. You gentlemen must be as tired as I. Smythe, go home to your wife. Tomorrow will prove to be a trying day for both of you. Edmond, I won't need you again tonight, you may retire."

By HALF-NINE the following morning as Harry sat in his office drinking his second cup of coffee, he cringed at what was occurring across town in Smythe's office. Since Smythe was the head of the runner's, the Secretary of War himself would cause a scene by firing Smythe. No charges would be brought against him, but it would be widely known he was a suspect in the two murders of War Office officials. Harry felt bad for doing this to Smythe and bringing him on board. If in the future, he changed his mind about working for the War Office, they would plan for him to retake his post. Somehow, Harry didn't think he would go back. Smythe had that look in his eyes last night after finding out about Kincaid and James. He already felt attached to them and the War Office. If only there were more good, determined, and fearless men like him. England would benefit immensely for it.

When SMYTHE ARRIVED home in the wee hours of the morning, instead of climbing back in bed with his lovely bride,

Mary Smythe, formally Miss Mary Spencer, he stoked the fire in their modest bedchamber and sat down in one of two newly upholstered chairs and contemplated how to explain to Mary about the events which would unfold when he arrived at work. Breaking her heart and causing her pain wasn't an option.

"Robert, has something happened? Why aren't you in bed?" His wife's voice, soft and sleepy, never failed to ease his heart. Nor awaken his body's desire for her.

"Why don't you join me. I've something to discuss with you." Wrapped in the bed's coverlet, she curled up on his lap, put her arms around his neck, and rested her head on his chest. Directly over his heart. A heart that belonged to her. He folded her in his arms and held her. Some days he could not believe how lucky he was to have married Mary. Because of who he was and who Mary was, the granddaughter of a countess, he never expected the marriage to be allowed to take place. It was the happiest day of his life. And not all that long ago.

"The War Office contacted me and offered me a position."

"Mmmm."

"Did you hear me?"

"Sorry. Still sleepy. Can you repeat what you said, my love?"

"The War Office contacted me and offered me a position."

"Congratulations. That is quite an honor, is it not?"

"It is."

Her arms slipped from his neck, and she sat up, looking at him with sleepy eyes. "Then why is there no excitement in your voice?"

"In order to make my undercover work as a spy plausible, my reputation as a Runner has to be ruined. Tomorrow morning, they will fire me as the head of the Bow Street

Runners, claiming I'm a suspect in the murder of two gentlemen."

"I don't understand?"

"I'm going undercover for the War Office to catch an English Lord who works for the French. Has worked for them for years, even during the war. I need to re-establish myself into the rookeries and back alleys of St. Giles. I need people to trust me with their secrets, so I can help bring to justice this Englishman. Also, two of the War Office's spies were murdered last night." He paused and waited for Mary to comprehend what he'd just said.

"I thought you said after we wed, you would take a less dangerous role within the Runners."

She remembered correctly. "I was planning on it. I never imagined working for the War Office. They came to me. How can I turn down a position that the prince sent someone to offer me?"

"I don't suppose you can."

"No, sweetheart, I can't. You need to listen to me. I told you because it will ruin my name and reputation."

She gasped.

"You are the only one I'm allowed, at this point in time, to confide in. In order to keep you from being ruined as well, you'll have to move home temporarily with Spencer and Miranda. Or go and stay with Elizabeth and Amesbury." He hugged her close and kissed the top of her head. "I'm so sorry for what this will do to you. If I could, in some way, prevent this ugliness I would. However, because of all the Crown has done for me, I need to give back."

He moved, so they faced each other. His hands cupped her cheeks, which were wet with tears, and his heart cracked in two. "I love you. No matter what you hear or your family tells you to do, I love you. Nothing bad about me that reaches your ears is true. Remember that. Remember in your heart who I am. Loyal, honorable, and trustworthy. And most of all, I love you with all my heart." Robert couldn't say it surprised him to feel tears pooling in his eyes. He hated to cause Mary pain. And even though she would know the truth, she would be hurt by all the hurtful comments made to her about him. If only he could save and protect her from what was about to happen. "Perhaps you should retire to Bath for a spell. That way you will not be subjected to hurt and scandal firsthand."

"No. At least not in the beginning." Hurt and worry radiated from her eyes. Eyes he never wanted to see anything but happiness in. Perhaps he'd made a terrible mistake in accepting Newbury's offer. It had only been a brief time since he needed to remember he didn't just have himself to concern himself with. He now had a wife he adored and loved beyond reason and his decision in joining the War Office would affect her as much, if not more, than him.

"I believe I will stay with Elizabeth and Amesbury, if they don't mind."

"They would never refuse your desire to spend time with them. Besides, Amesbury's London townhome is large enough you would not infringe on their privacy at all." He looked deep into her eyes, hoping all the love and desire he had for her shined through. He kissed her deeply, setting off an explosion of need. Picking her up, he carried her to bed and made love to her until the sun awoke, kissing the sky with its bright yellow and orange rays signaling another day of life. As his beloved wife slumbered in his arms, he prayed she would forgive him for what was to come. Because even he couldn't comprehend how bad the fallout would be for her. He didn't care what people thought or said about him. His worry centered on Mary and keeping her safe from harm and the hurtful wagging tongues of the ton.

# CHAPTER 7

"He what?" Penelope must have heard Thomas wrong.

"I'm sorry. His Grace has sent a missive saying he has to postpone the wedding due to unforeseen circumstances. And hopes you understand that he is not breaking off the engagement." Her brother's eyes narrowed to slits; his anger palpable within the four walls. "If he cancels, I'll have him murdered. The bloody bastard, 'unforeseen circumstances' my arse. He better come up with something better when I pay him an unannounced call this afternoon. This could ruin you. If I could get my hands on his neck?" Penelope cringed as he used his hands and pretended to strangle someone. It almost made her feel sorry for Newbury.

"Why don't I call it off and be done with him."

"No," he bellowed.

"If I call off our engagement, there will be talk, but no scandal and I will not be ruined. Which means so much to you." She waved her hand. "The announcement will not come as a shock when you consider whom I'm affianced to."

He went silent and Penelope could see by the light in his eyes he was thinking on it.

"Perhaps Mr. Sinclair would be willing to marry you. After all, you come with a large dowry. Not that I've heard anything good or bad about his finances. He is also next in line to inherit should Newbury croak." He paused and looked at her with renewed interest.

The idea of marrying Mr. Sinclair had her insides in an uproar. She wouldn't lie and say she didn't find him interesting and more than handsome. However, she found Newbury brought out the same thoughts. "Seeing's how Mr. Sinclair and Newbury are the only relatives each man has; I refuse to cause a rift between them. Marrying Mr. Sinclair is not an option."

"Fine. But I'm paying a visit to Newbury today nonetheless."

HOLED up in his study for hours awaiting Smythe's arrival, Harry had ideas and plans jotted down on paper scattered all over his usually impeccably neat desktop. His thoughts kept swinging back and forth between the murders of his colleagues and his postponement of his wedding. After sending a message to Wentworth that morning, he'd heard nothing. He expected a scathing remark from the affable, well-liked and admired, duke.

"Excuse me, Your Grace," the butler, Greeves, said as he entered the study and bowed. "Mr. Smythe has arrived."

"Thank you."

Smythe walked in, clothes and hair mussed and the man's eyes huge with shock."

"Sit. You look like hell."

"I feel like hell, even worse." He collapsed into a chair and closed his eyes."

"Here, take this." Harry had expected his stressful arrival and had a glass of whiskey waiting.

The ex-Runner's eyes popped open. "Thank you. I believe I need several more of these to numb my brain." He downed the glass, coughed, and held it out. "Another, please."

Harry filled the glass to the brim this time and went around his desk and sat. His hand picked up his own glass and took a long sip and enjoyed the heat as it went down his throat and coated his stomach. "Was it that bad?"

Smythe's entire body shuttered as he wisely sipped his drink. "Worse. The disbelief and then hatred on the faces of those I've worked with for years shocked me. I expected some loyalty to me for all I've done."

"How did your wife handle it when you told her what would happen?"

His eyes lowered and focused on the glass clutched in his hand. "She is worried for me. She's a wise and remarkable woman for someone so young as eight and ten. We agreed she would stay with her sister, the Marchioness of Amesbury, for the foreseeable future."

Discussing Smythe's young wife had Harry's mind conjuring up Penelope's lovely face. How, when she smiled, it lit up her blue eyes the color of the midday sky. She must be furious with him for postponing their marriage.

"Excuse me again, Your Grace, but the Duke of Wentworth is here to see you. I explained you were not receiving visitors, but he insists upon speaking with you. You must quickly get on your disguise."

No sooner had the valet finished speaking, did Wentworth barge into the room.

Harry stood and rounded the desk. "See here, Wentworth."

Wentworth looked from Smythe, who he acknowledged with a nod, and then Newbury. "Sinclair?" He frowned and paused for several long drawn out moments. "Did the valet just call you, Your Grace?" His eyes flew from Smythe to him and back to Smythe. "Who is this man to you?"

Harry knew the two men were friends. They may not have started out that way in the beginning when Wentworth hired the Runner to work for him, but over the years they became close friends. Smythe looked to him with a cocked brow and resigned look. "I'll let him answer."

Blue eyes, very close to Penelope's, pierced into his. Only a violent storm brewed in these. Destined to kill anyone in its path. "I'll explain all if you'll please take a seat."

Wentworth took the seat beside Smythe with a huff, never taking his eyes off Harry. Until Harry broke the contact by turning his back and pouring the duke a nearly full glass of whiskey. It gave him time to arrange in his mind how he would explain the deception.

"Here. I find myself repeating the words I spoke already once today. You will need this." Harry sat down in his desk chair and faced the two men. "I apologize to you Smythe for having to witness this."

The Runner looked amused. "I find myself needing a diversion from my own problems. No need to apologize."

"Yes, well. Here's goes. What I say to you, Wentworth, is confidential. It will put many peoples' lives in danger, including Smythe's, if you repeat anything I'm about to share with you. I work for the War Office. I am a close adviser to the prince. I work undercover, which is why I have two identities. I am the Duke of Newbury. Hugh Sinclair does not exist."

He waited and watched Wentworth closely. The duke knew how to hide his genuine emotions. Quick as anything he jumped up and swung his fist. Harry saw it coming, reached out and deflected the punch. Wentworth swung with his other arm, landing a punch to his upper cheek. Not with enough force that Newbury's head snapped back but hard enough that his eye stung and he could feel it swelling.

"For bloody sake, Wentworth, sit down."

Shockingly, he did. "Damn Newbury. You made a bloody fool of my sister and me. Did you enjoy it? Have a good laugh at our expense? When were you going to reveal your true self to Penelope? After the vows were spoken and the marriage consummated, making her stuck with a liar for life? Do you honestly believe she would have forgiven you for deceiving her? I see the way she looks at you and Sinclair. She has feelings for both of them...you...and no doubt is having terrible guilt over it. You are causing her much stress and anxiety. I'll not have it last another day. If you wish to wed Lady Penelope, you must end this deception today." He paused, raked both his hands through his light hair, closed his eyes, and looked resigned. "I can't believe I debated calling off the wedding and considered betrothing my sister to Sinclair?"

It was hard for Harry not to be stabbed with guilt for his deception. He couldn't say he hadn't thought about the repercussions when he finally told Penelope about his double life. He had. And he knew it would cause a rift between them for a time. He only hoped he could win back her favor when she realized they shared a love most married couples never found.

Love? Did he love her? He desired her beyond reason. Dreamed about her. Thought about her during the most inopportune times. Was it love? He believed so. Now, what to do about it?

"Smythe, do you mind giving Wentworth and me some privacy?" Wentworth, the man he thought silly for openly loving his wife, and here was Harry admitting to loving Penelope. Perhaps there was something to marriages based on love.

"No," Wentworth barked. "I have no secrets from Smythe

and trust him with my life and the lives of all those I care for."

Harry sighed with resolve. "As you wish. But before I continue, you must know something. Smythe now works for the War Office directly under me. You will hear things about him today. About him being fired from the Runners and accused of murder. All false in order to set up his work with me. He left the Runners with an impeccable record and loyalty and is not accused of murdering anyone. Nothing said between us today can be divulged to anyone. Swear it and your elegance to the Crown."

"I swear it." He didn't hesitate. Harry liked a man who knew his mind.

"Thank you." He held up the decanter of whiskey. "Would either of you care for more drink?"

Smythe shook his head. "I cannot speak for Wentworth, but you have managed to dull my wits."

"Not mine," Wentworth said, "continue."

Harry raised a brow on being ordered, not asked. Wentworth clearly had forgotten they held the same title. Since he didn't go for formality or title most of the time, he ignored it. "The few who know of my dual personalities, the better. Actually, I have four. But the other two I will not share with you. Only those who work with me closely know them. If I want to live long enough to have a wife and family, it needs to stay that way. Also, no matter what is being said about Smythe, you may say nothing. I know it will be difficult, especially when your close circle of friends get together to discuss the issue."

"Excuse me?" Wentworth eyed him defensively.

"Please. I know Spencer will seek out Bridgeton, who is his close cousin, and you, Myles and Amesbury for counsel. Spencer will want to kill Smythe with his bare hands, and you will convince him otherwise without giving away his secrets. Can I rely on you to do this?"

Unfortunately, Harry couldn't get a read on Wentworth. But he knew he could trust him to do what was right.

"You can rely on me. If we have to lock Spencer up, we will to keep him from going after Smythe. Trust me when I say he saw first-hand what Newgate is like and what it did to Bridgeton." He winced. "Not my proudest moment having Bridgeton thrown in the bowels of hell for attempting to kill my sister, Lady Amelia. Which of course, as we all know, he didn't do. The blasted brother of his dead sister-in-law did. I'll remind Spencer that going to prison for life, or worse, being hung for murder, is not worth killing Smythe for. I'll convince him that within a month Smythe will be dead on the streets, anyway."

"Jeez. Thanks for your concern, Wentworth," Smythe drawled. "I thought you were a loyal friend."

Wentworth chuckled. "You know I am. And I'll watch your back anytime you need me to. Now that you have successfully diverted the subject away from my sister, Newbury, may we return to what you intend to do about her."

"I still intend to marry her. There is a dire case I'm working on, which needs to be solved quickly. I can't leave for even two days to get married."

"I'll make a deal," Wentworth began. "Instead of the vows taking place at Stoney Cross Manor in a fortnight, they take place at Wentworth House in two days."

"But…"

"Hear me out." Wentworth held up his hand. "If you agree, I promise to help you smooth over the war, that will happen, when Penelope finds out about your deception."

"Deal." It was the best Harry could hope for. His marriage to Penelope would take place. He would worry about the rest when the time came. Saying the vows and consummating those vows were his priority as the Duke of Newbury.

Wentworth stood. "Then I think my time here is concluded." He turned back to Smythe. "One more thing. Does Mary know? I would hate for her to be kept in the dark and her heart broken."

"She knows. And we decided the best thing for her was to stay with Elizabeth and Amesbury for a time."

"Good. Even with her knowing the truth, it won't be easy for her. People are ruthless. I hope she intends to stay indoors until this settles. Which brings up something else? How will it be settled?"

"Smythe's name will be cleared and he'll be offered his position back as the head of the Bow Street Runners, which he will decline. We will give him a fictitious job title working for the Crown. Meanwhile, he will continue working for me under the guise of a new identity. As all spies have."

"I can see myself out. Good luck to both of you. You will need it."

"Well, that went better than I thought," Harry said, not referring to Smythe's dilemma but to his.

"Yes. Well. Your problems are nothing compared to mine."

"You are correct. I don't think it's wise for you to return to your home. I'll send one of my men to collect some of your belongings and you will stay here. I have a trusted acquaintance of the theater who will come tomorrow to work on your disguise as a Mr. Walter Temple. Not even your wife will recognize you when he is done. Meanwhile, you will not leave this house. It's for your protection."

"I understand."

"I've had rooms prepared for you. My housekeeper, Mrs. Mere, will show you to them."

~

"He, what?" It was the second time today she asked that of her brother.

"Since he can't get away for the wedding as we had planned, he asked if the ceremony could take place here in two days."

"I refuse." How dare Newbury keep toying with her emotions by changing things for his convenience? Her insides could not take much more change. What little food she'd consumed today hadn't settled well as it was. And now!

"You can't refuse." Her brother looked at her with compassion. "I already agreed. I have notified a local clergy. Sent word to your seamstress telling her there would be a large bonus if she delivers your dress the day after tomorrow by noon. I've sent word to Mother, Sebastian, and Teagan in Scotland, but they can never arrive in time. All our other guests know of the change."

In two days time, she would become the Duchess of Newbury, whether or not she wanted to. She may as well resign herself to the inevitable. "May I retire to my room?"

"Penelope. Someday I hope you will forgive me and know I did what I thought was best for you."

Inside her rooms, her maid helped her strip down to her chemise and tucked her into bed. A nap was all she had the energy for. They were due to attend a small intimate dinner at her sister, Bella's, that evening. Her maid would deliver the hastily penned missive to Wentworth saying she was unwell and to please make her excuses to Bella. The earl and countess of Northborough had a marriage made from love, respect, and admiration. She groaned and hugged her stomach. As with all the Seabrook family members, love came in their marriage, but it came at a price. Bella, at one point, had given up on Myles asking for her hand in marriage and used Stuart Spencer to make Myles jealous.

Thomas and Emma had their differences in the beginning. It was known that Thomas kept secrets from her about her father, Mr. Hamilton. But eventually love won.

Amelia and William Spencer, the Count and Countess of Bridgeton. Amelia's dead betrothed, and a child born out of wedlock. A murdered brother and sister-in-law of Bridgeton's, blamed on him but never proven. Time in Newgate for Bridgeton, but ultimately, the two wed and lived in wedded bliss.

Which brought her to her brother, Sebastian. He set out on horseback to Northern England to find her and take her back to London. On his travels, thieves accosted him and left him for dead. Teagan and Lachlan Murray, running for their lives from their father, found him and nursed him back to health. When the Murrays' father got word they were alive, he sent his men to finish the job. Teagan, Lachlan, and Sebastian fled to London and the safety of Wentworth's household. By the time they reached London, Teagan and Sebastian were already in love and wed not long after.

Over and over and over her half-siblings married for love. Moans escaped her lips as her stomachache refused to abate. How could she love Newbury when she felt something for Mr. Sinclair? If Mr. Sinclair were out of the picture, and not a temptation, surely her heart would belong to the duke exclusively.

Visions of both of them entered her mind. She closed her eyes tight, hoping to quell the handsome half-face of the duke and the whole face of Mr. Sinclair. They needed to leave her alone. She needed to sleep and pray when she awoke she would be ready to face her future as the Duchess of Newbury. She—a bastard daughter of a duke and his mistress—becoming a duke's wife. As sleep pulled her under, the last thing she saw was the merging of the two men as they become one.

# CHAPTER 8

RIGHT AFTER LUNCHEON, ON THE DAY OF HER WEDDING, Penelope found herself dressed in her wedding gown of the palest yellow silk trimmed with cream. It had a shockingly low neckline and a high waist trimmed in cream satin ribbon. The silk skirt draped unadorned to the floor and thankfully her petticoat kept the silk skirt from clinging to her legs. The seamstress was nipping and tucking, making last-minute alterations to the gown. When the seamstress finally declared she was done and forced Penelope to look into the mirror she gasped. As if the gown wasn't beautiful enough, there was a matching cloak, yellow silk slippers, long gloves made with the same silk fabric. The gown made her look like a princess. And she was the farthest thing from a princess.

"It's beautiful. More than beautiful," Emma said with a smile. "I think it's the loveliest gown I've ever seen."

Penelope beamed into the mirror. Even without her hair dressed with flowers for adornment, she looked beautiful. It was hard to recognize herself beneath all the finery. "It's perfect," she declared to the seamstress who appeared to be waiting anxiously for some reaction.

Once the dressmaker and her assistant left, Penelope's maid, Clarisse, entered. "Lady Penelope, you look beautiful. Please take a seat at the vanity so I can do your hair? In no time you will descend the staircase to marry your duke."

Before Penelope sat, Emma gave her a kiss on the cheek. "I've never seen a lovelier bride. Now I need to prepare. Until later."

Penelope wore her long blonde tresses up with loose curls cascading down across one shoulder. Daisies, which were her favorite flower, in white and yellow were tucked here and there, adding a whimsical look to her. Emma lent her small diamond drop earrings and a matching delicate diamond necklace.

"I declare, Lady Penelope," Clarisse said as she made last-minute touches to her hair. "No more beautiful bride ever existed. I predict the duke, the one you are marrying, will forget how to breathe when he sets eyes on you. The duke, your brother that is, informed me he would collect you promptly at two."

"I'd like a few minutes alone."

Her maid curtsied. "Yes, milady."

Penelope rose up from her chair at the dressing table, stood in front of the full-length mirror, and peered into the looking glass, trying to find herself in the reflection reflected back at her. If she looked close enough, she could see the girl from the northern country in the depths of her blue eyes. Bright, wide eyes full of wonder and nervous excitement. *In an hour I will become the Duke of Newbury's Duchess. Tonight he will come to my bed and make me his.*

A knock on the door startled her. "Come in."

Wentworth entered the room, and when he looked at her, he stopped dead. "You look beautiful. Newbury is a fortunate man. Now I will say something I told Bella and Amelia before they wed. If you ever need me for anything, be it trivial or major, all you need do is send for me. I will always be your brother and will always look out for you."

Penelope blinked back tears. "Thank you."

He held out his arm. "Shall we?"

She smiled, took a deep inhale and exhale to steady her nerves, and placed her hand on his forearm. "We shall."

The first thing Penelope noticed when she entered the drawing room on her brother's arm was her family sitting in chairs on either side of the room, making an aisle for her to walk down. A very short aisle, but an aisle nonetheless, and tears pooled in her eyes at their thoughtfulness. After smiling and dipping her head to her family and friends, she forced herself to look at the end of the path and the man standing there with the clergy.

Newbury looked dashing dressed in formal wear, making her almost trip. Seeing him now, dressed in black with a starched white shirt and impeccably tied black cravat, breeches tucked into black Hessians—no heeled dress shoes for this duke—he resembled most every other member of the ton. Except for a few details. His black patch, which, not for the first time, made him appear mysterious. The scar, which never seemed to heal, only added a dangerous flair. She could almost forget about his leg as he stood straight, barely leaning on his cane. It also helped that it was black as well. The only thing noticeable was the silver lion's head, which his hand gripped.

His lips curled up into a smile that caused his one eye to sparkle. Her stomach fluttered as she realized he wanted to marry her. Was happy about the union. She reached the end of the aisle, curtsied to her brother. Turned to Newbury, curtsied deep, and said, "Your Grace."

He reached out, taking her hand as she rose, and he

bowed. His gaze never left hers as he raised her gloved hand up and brushed his lips across her knuckles. "Milady."

The clergy opened an ancient tome. "We shall begin."

Newbury and Penelope faced one other, both hands joined.

The ceremony passed in a blur. When the clergy pronounced them man and wife, duke and duchess, Newbury gently pressed his lips to hers as their witnesses cheered and congratulated them.

They skipped the traditional wedding breakfast for an early evening meal. The newlyweds sat across from each other at the end of the table with Wentworth at the head. The two men discussed several topics including government, the recent riots by the factory workers, and The House of Lords. Things she didn't have any interest in, except for the children working in sweatshops. Children should not be working in such deplorable conditions for sixteen-hour days with little pay. She'd heard stories about the doors being locked from the outside so no one could leave until they were opened. About a fire in one textile factory where every single person perished. Oh dear, it was her wedding day. She best think happy thoughts or she'd have her family worried about the frown and concerned emotions on her face.

Voices traveled around the long rectangular table. Laughter and chuckles made their way to her ears. Emma, Bella, Myles, and Amelia appeared engrossed in a humorous conversation. While Spenser, Bridgeton, and Mary—where was Mary's husband—spoke softly about something serious, if looks were any sign. Miranda, Elizabeth, and Amesbury were alternating between serious and joy. Penelope didn't know what she felt. She picked at her food until they served the next course, and she picked more. Nerves jingled inside her stomach, and she didn't want to have a stomachache the night of her wedding. Her heart hurt a little, as though it didn't know what to feel. One moment it was beating fast, then the next it eased only to speed up once again.

It equaled the contradiction of her feelings for Newbury. One moment she found herself unable to take her eyes off him, his handsomeness and over-all charm mesmerizing. And the next, she'd conjure up what his injured eye looked like beneath the patch. A grotesque, empty hole where his eyeball should be. A black nothing. And a leg crisscrossed with raised scars running up and down the entire length. His kneecap twisted to the side.

It wasn't good to let her mind run wild while attending her wedding meal. She never considered herself a shallow person. Had not been brought up privileged. Had seen her share of injuries both from the war and from being in service. Never thought less of a person because of limitations. She did not think less of Newbury because of his. In fact, she admired him and believed she was drawn to him because of those limitations.

As far as tonight. She lowered her head as heat blossomed on her cheeks. Something she didn't want her husband to see. She didn't want him thinking she was thinking about him. Even if she was. Being raised with servants and the lecherous viscount, Penelope had seen her share of couples fornicating. So tonight would not be a surprise. And if she were afraid of seeing the duke naked, she would insist on total darkness. No candles, no coals glowing in the hearth. Complete and utter darkness. Thinking about the dark had her heart easing and her insides settling somewhat.

"My dear." Newbury stood beside her chair with his hand out. So lost in her own thoughts, she'd not heard or seen him approach. "I believe it's time I escort you to your new home."

Oh, God! Instant panic. Her eyes darted around the table as everyone wished them, "Good evening." Wentworth spoke to her, and she heard nothing but the pounding in her ears.

She placed her hand in her husband's—stood on wobbly legs, praying they supported her and she didn't end up in a heap of yellow on the floor—and he led her down the stairs. They retrieved his overcoat, hat, and gloves and her cloak and hat from the doorman.

Once settled inside the black carriage with the Newbury ducal crest, Penelope's new husband draped a soft blanket over her lap. "I realized today that you have never seen Newbury House."

"No, I haven't."

"It's close to Wentworth Manor on Piccadilly. During the past several years, since becoming duke, I've spent little time looking at or thinking about the décor. My housekeeper, Mrs. Mere, will be the first to say the house needs updating. Just say the word and I will have the house inundated with decorators and carpenters."

"That's very generous of you."

"See, we have arrived."

Indeed, they had, and her eyes widened at the home. Even in the shadow of darkness she got the impression of a large, stately manor. It would be nice to see it in the light of day.

"What is your first impression?"

"Large."

Deep throaty laughter bounced around the carriage. "That it is." The driver opened the door, let down the steps. He held out his hand to Newbury, and he waved him off. "I can manage myself." Penelope tried not to worry that even one misstep would have him tumbling to the crushed stone granite of the drive. She sighed with relief when he landed, turned toward her and held up his hand. "Your Grace."

Their hands touched, both covered with gloves, and yet it was as though the contact was bare skin to bare skin. "Thank you, Your Grace."

"Would you like an introduction to the staff tonight or in the morning when you're refreshed from sleep?"

Sleep? Would she be able to sleep? "The morning would be wonderful."

"Morning it is."

After removing his overcoat, hat, and gloves, helping her with her cloak and hat, Newbury escorted her up a beautiful wooden staircase with intricate wrought-iron railings. At the top it curved, veering off in two directions. They headed to the right and near the end of the hallway he opened a large wooden door with a curved top. "These are your rooms. I hope they're to your liking. I believe your maid has arrived and unpacked your things. I've ordered a small tray to be sent up in an hour. I hope that's sufficient time before I join you?"

"Yes."

"Then I will leave you to your privacy."

Penelope entered the room, and Newbury closed the door after her. The room glowed under the candlelight, highlighting the shades of blue and cream. It wasn't overly feminine, nor masculine. Somewhere in the middle and Penelope found she liked it. There was an enormous tester bed in mahogany against a wall with small tables on each side. There was a rather extensive wardrobe and a perfect-sized writing desk, which would serve as her dressing table as well. Clarisse had already placed her brush and hand-held mirror on the polished wood. In the far corner stood a privacy screen. On the back wall, a brick fireplace roared with flames. The room had the chill and dampness indicative of being closed up for far too long.

She was just about to explore her sitting room behind the French doors when her maid entered carrying a box. "I've brought you a gift from the Duchess of Wentworth." She placed the box on the blue and cream paisley coverlet.

Penelope's fingers gently removed the cover, spread the tissue paper to the side, and she gasped. With trembling hands, she removed a thin, nearly see-through pale yellow night rail and matching robe. The linen fabric was the softest she'd ever felt. There was only one problem, she would be nearly naked wearing it. Newbury would be able to see... everything. Obviously, Emma's plan. What a naughty sister-in-law she had. Tears sprang to her eyes. She missed her already. How would she ever survive living here without her newfound-family? She drew her strength from them on a daily basis.

"Your Grace." Clarisse handed her one of her mono-grammed handkerchiefs. "May I assist you in preparing for bed?"

Penelope couldn't find her voice as tears clogged her throat. Ever since she first became betrothed to Newbury, she'd become a watering pot. And she didn't like it one bit. "If you'll undo the back of my gown, I can manage the rest and you may retire for the evening."

Clarisse began the tedious task of unbuttoning all the tiny seed pearl buttons. "There, every last one unbuttoned. There is fresh, warm water, soap and towels behind the screen." She curtsied. "Good night, Your Grace."

"Good night." Her time of reckoning had come. She removed her lovely wedding dress and painstakingly hung it up in her wardrobe. She removed her petticoat, chemise, and pantaloons, draped them on a chair and hurried behind the screen to wash up. "Drat, I left my night clothes on the bed," she said out loud. Wrapped in a towel she made her way to the bed and quickly slid the night rail over her head, did up the laces and swore she'd felt nothing finer against her naked skin. Next came the beautiful robe. It had a string that tied at the neck. She moved to the full-length mirror, her eyes bugging out of her head. "This won't do," she murmured.

"My nipples are showing and the patch of hair between my legs." She walked to the wardrobe, threw open the doors, and grabbed a white wrap. She swung it around her shoulders, letting one side hang longer than the other. She looked into the mirror again. "Better."

"What's better, my dear?"

Startled, she spun around and found her husband standing in the doorway grinning at her. He'd changed as well. Wore trousers and a loose-fitting shirt that went over the head and tied in the front. Only the top of his shirt wasn't tied closed, it was open, showing his chest, sprinkled with dark hair. She swallowed when she glimpsed his bare feet. Using his cane, he hobbled her way. "I ask again. What's better?"

"Nothing." She stood there not knowing what to do with her hands, or any other part of her body.

"A tray has arrived. It's in my sitting room." He pointed his cane. "Please join me."

"I was just about to undress my hair."

His one eye narrowed, and he looked inquisitively at her. "Allow me."

Penelope sat at her dressing table and stared into the reflection in the looking glass as one by one Newbury pulled the real flowers from her hair. Each slightly wilted petal made its way to his nose where he inhaled. When the flowers were gone, he plucked the pins. His hands were surprisingly gentle and adept. When her hair fell to her waist, he spread his fingers through it, seeking any pins he'd missed. The whole time he worked, her head tingled. Her eyes followed every move his large hands made. When he declared he'd gotten all the pins out, he picked up her brush and ever-so-gently stroked it through her hair. Her eyes were riveted to his hands as he worked the tangles out of her hair and then brushed it to a lovely sheen.

"Done."

When he stepped back, she missed his attention. He'd awakened her body, and she felt flushed from head to toe. "Thank you. You obviously have experience brushing ladies' hair." The moment the words escaped her lips, she wished them back. It was their wedding night. She shouldn't be bringing up other women. "I'm sorry."

Their eyes connected in the mirror. Her two, his one. For a second she thought she saw sadness, then he blinked, and it was gone. "No need to be sorry for speaking your mind. And the truth is I have experience with helping ladies undress their hair for bed."

HE COULDN'T JUST LET her comment about undressing hair go? His words hurt her. He could see it plain as day in her blue eyes. When he brushed her hair, her eyes had a dreamy, intimate look to them. She may not have realized it, but her wrap had fallen away, revealing her nipples through the thin fabric. His body responded, his cock hardening. And all he could think about was covering her body with his and entering her. Being inside her.

And then she mentioned him having experience brushing ladies' hair, and it broke the spell. He wasn't angry at her but at himself for saying something hurtful. When the truth was, he'd never brushed another person's hair before. He lashed out because the gorgeous, delicate woman he married made him nervous.

As he escorted her to the small table set up in the sitting room, he tried to keep his eyes averted from her exposed body. Who in bloody hell would give a virgin on her wedding night a see through night rail and robe was beyond him. He would like to thank the person and ring their neck at the same time. Sitting opposite Penelope now as he was, was sheer torture to his over-sensitive emotions. The surrounding air clashed with awareness. Neither of them ate much. Just picked at their food and sipped the wine.

"Is your room to your liking?" If he didn't start a conversation, his head would explode.

Moments ticked by as her lovely blue eyes widened over the rim of the crystal goblet. "Yes. Very much so."

"If there is anything you need, please ask. This is your home now."

Her eyes dropped to her hands, which rested beneath the table. "I will."

Conversation with Penelope was difficult in most circumstances when they were alone together, but tonight proved even more so. She was his wife, his duchess. His to do with as he so pleased. So why was he hesitating taking her to bed? Rising, he held out his hand. "My dear, shall we retire for the evening?" His voice sounded strange to his own ears. What must she be thinking?

Eyes downcast, she whispered, "Yes."

Entering her chamber, he led her to the large bed dominating the room, all the while wishing he could know what went on inside her head. Was she nervous? Afraid? Relieved? Only one way to find out.

Pausing beside the bed, he turned Penelope so she faced him. Resting his cane against the bedpost, he spread his hands on her soft, flush cheeks and lowered his lips to hers. She tasted as he remembered from their previous kisses. Sweet, soft, and fruity like the wine. After a time, he slipped his tongue inside her mouth and moaned as heat burned throughout his body. One hand moved into her thick glorious hair and the other to the small of her back, pulling her forward so his hips cradled her.

She gasped, or moaned, making him pause until her arms

wrapped around his neck and she joined in the kiss. This time she took the lead. Her tongue explored, her teeth nipped, her hands clutched his hair. Christ, she devoured him, causing his knees to weaken.

≈

PENELOPE GASPED for air between Harry's lips. In the past, his kisses had been wonderful. Tonight they went beyond wonderful. Every nerve ending in her being tingled with awareness from his kisses. Kisses she knew were meant to seduce. He was seducing her on their wedding night. Perfectly fine with her. The sooner they consummated their vows, the better. Except, she wasn't in a hurry, her mind and body languidly enjoyed his loving ministrations. The gentle brush of his fingertips here and there. The feel of his lips against hers and the softness of his tongue inside her mouth had her reveling in the here and now, and she never wanted the feelings to end. This excitement, contentment, and need all jumbled up inside her was euphoric.

"You are beautiful," Harry murmured into her ear as his hands untied her robe and it slithered to the floor. Before she comprehended what he would do next, her night rail joined her robe. Naked and vulnerable, she clutched his shoulders, hoping to hide her nakedness from him. It was one thing for her maid to see her thus, but Harry?

"There is no need for you to hide from me. I'm your husband."

With eyes wide with shock and interest, Penelope stepped back, wrapped her arms across her bare breasts and stood mesmerized as Harry undressed. His capable hands slid his shirt up and over his head, revealing a hard, strong chest and shoulder muscles. His long fingers unbuttoned the front placket to his trousers, and Penelope held her breath. Heart pounding, body shaking, her eyes riveted to his fingers as he pulled his trousers and undergarment down and off his body, leaving him naked before her. His lame leg was no hindrance to the act of unclothing. She couldn't see much of his knee because of the brace he wore, but it didn't look hideous or disfigured.

It wasn't the first time she'd eyed a naked man. But this man was Harry, her husband, and by his swollen and hard member she would presume he was ready to consummate their marriage. She cleared her throat, trying to speak, but nothing would exit. Instead, she gasped, turned, and climbed beneath the coverlet.

He chuckled. He actually chuckled as he pulled back the covers and joined her in the bed. As he did so, his side of the bed dipped beneath his weight, causing her to slide toward him ever so slightly.

"What are you laughing about," she huffed as she fluffed up her pillows and sat with the coverlet up to her chin for protection.

"You, turning your back on me and hiding beneath the covers." He fluffed his pillows and sat. Only he let the covers fall to his waist. "I saw all there is to see. You are beautiful and need not hide from me. Besides," he grinned, "when you turned you gave me a perfect view of your backside."

She wanted to smack him with one of her pillows, but she remained still. At least her body remained still. Her insides burned, which then heated her skin.

"Blushing becomes you, my dear."

"Stop it."

"Stop what?"

"Just do your husbandly duty so I may sleep."

Disappointment flashed in his one eye before he grinned and took her mouth in a kiss meant to curl toes and cause ladies to lift their skirts. Before she knew it, she was kissing him back with abandon and sighing and moaning as his hands roamed her body. When he cupped her there, her breath stalled and then she panted as his fingers played with her. Her hips rose off the bed, noises escaped her lips, and her legs opened wider, seeking some elusive release. As it crashed into her, she screamed as she shook her head from side to side, fighting and enjoying the sensations bombarding her body. Shocked at her behavior, she pushed Harry away and curled up on her side, trying to hide. Trying to find covers to cover her nakedness.

"Easy, Penelope. There's no need to hide from me. What just happened to you is wonderful. It proves something I knew about you from the start. You are a sensual woman, and our relationship in the bedroom will be anything but boring. "Please." He touched her shoulder. "Turn around and let me hold you. Let me love you properly."

Swallowing her mortification, Penelope rolled onto her back. Harry took advantage and wrapped his arms around her and tugged her so she lay half on top of his chest and half on the bed.

He exhaled. "Much better."

Words escaped her. She nodded her head in agreement. Because being held within his strong, warm arms made her feel safe, cherished and, if not loved, at least appreciated. Perhaps love between them would come in time. Truth be told, she was halfway in love with Harry already. Would he? Could he ever love her? There was no time to ponder the question as his hands began roaming her body, and Penelope's inner sensual being started taking over her mind and body.

Harry moved over her, and she took the time to study his face. Really study it by the flicker of light coming off the flames from the fireplace. Her eyes moved around his face, but when she returned to his good eye, the soft blue glowed.

He looked young, handsome and relaxed. She hardly noticed the scar down his left side, nor the black patch she was becoming accustomed to. Her insides tingled and her heart pitter-pattered inside her chest. Finally, he leaned down and took her lips in a kiss. Breaking it, he placed feather like kisses down her neck, across her chest, and up the other side.

His knee nudged her legs apart, and his hand played with her, causing her breath to catch and her hips to squirm. Now that her body knew what would come, it wanted to feel those sensations again. He rose up, took his member in his hand, placed it at her entrance, and pushed slow and steady. Again and again as her body adjusted to the size and invasion. One more push. Pain seared her insides, and she gasped.

"I'm sorry." Harry looked at her with compassion, then kissed the tip of her nose. "I believe the pain will subside momentarily."

Seeing the compassion in his eyes and him giving her a tender kiss on the nose had her heart tumbling again for this man who became her husband today. Before she could say the pain was easing, Harry began pulling in and out of her, causing her body to tighten around his member. The harder, the faster he moved, the more her inner body clamped around his sex until she clutched his hips, keeping him in place as her legs shook, her insides pulsated, and her head spun with what she now knew was sexual release.

Harry groaned, and his body tightened as he released his warm seed.

NOT WANTING TO SQUISH PENELOPE, Harry rolled off her onto his back and gasped for much-needed air. It took some time for his mind to catch up to his body, but when it did all he could do was smile. Life, this part of their married life, would be satisfying. His new wife would not close her eyes and think happy thoughts while he did his husbandly duties. No indeed. He was a fortunate man to have made such a wonderful match.

Outside the bedroom, they had much to learn about each other, but Harry also knew they would get along splendidly. Hadn't they already. And when he told her about being both Harry and Hugh, perhaps she would be relieved and not angry.

A sudden chill washed across his body. He adjusted the coverlet, so they were both covered. He leaned over and kissed Penelope lightly on the lips. "Thank you and good night." He would wait until she fell asleep before he left for his own bed. He couldn't risk falling asleep causing the make-up which created his scar to rub off or his patch to fall off. He knew he needed to confess all to her soon, but some niggling inside him told him to wait a while longer.

Her breath evened out and little snoring sounds escaped her lips, bringing a smile to his. Feeling as though he was invading her privacy, he left the warm bed, put on his clothes and entered his sitting room, poured himself a generous amount of brandy and sat in a chair by the fireplace which had burned down to hot coals and ash. He removed the brace from his knee, then bent and unbent it, hoping to work out the kinks. He removed his patch and blinked several times, adjusting to seeing out of two eyes instead of one. Using a handkerchief he wiped off his scar. Now that he and Penelope were living together it would prove difficult to keep his disguise secret. He would have to be Harry all day, every day. Not that he wasn't Harry all the time, he just wouldn't be able to go without his disguise. Not something he looked forward to. His leg got sore, his eye and cheek itched.

There was an alternative. Tell her the truth. Why did he fear the truth coming out? He would think it would relieve

Penelope to know she didn't marry a disfigured cripple. Perhaps over a private dinner tomorrow evening, he would tell her. Explain all that he could without divulging Crown secrets.

After the intimacy they shared this evening, she would forgive his deceit. He had to believe she would. The alternative was too painful to explore.

~

PENELOPE AWOKE to the curtains being drawn back from the windows, letting in cloud filtered sunlight.

"Good morning, Your Grace."

"Good morning, Clarisse. Would you leave and come back in an hour?

"Yes, Your Grace."

Once alone, Penelope curled onto her side and hugged herself. She couldn't stop the smile from forming on her lips as she remembered last night with Harry. How he made love to her with such gentleness and care for her comfort. Over the years, she'd heard stories about the marriage bed. How men could be cruel and violent to their wives. How they took their pleasure with no regard to their wife's. Her heart jumped. How fortunate for her to have married Harry. Never in her wildest imaginations had she ever thought to be anything more than a farmer's wife. And if she hadn't escaped Viscount Hadley, more likely his mistress and whore. Never a duchess.

After dressing in a comely sea-foam green day dress, her hair styled in a loose chignon, she made her way down the hallway, descended the stairs, and followed the smells making her stomach growl until she entered a cheery blue breakfast room. At the table sat her husband and their eyes connected, sending an inferno to her cheeks. Visions of last night flashed before her. How did intimate married people function on a day-to-day basis without embarrassment?

Emma, Bella, and Amelia never, well sometimes they did, blushed at something their husband's might whisper in their ear. Penelope, at this point, couldn't care less if her sisters and sister-in-law experienced mortification of deeds done in the marriage bed. Penelope cared about her and Harry and now, this very moment in the breakfast room, when moments ago her stomach growled and made known how little she'd eaten the day before. Only now, her stomach churned, and she felt dizzy and sick. Instead of fixing a plate, she made haste toward the opposite end of the cozy table and sat down with the help of a footman. Inhaling and exhaling, she willed her stomach and head to settle. Not to mention her emotions, which ran rampant the moment she saw Harry.

"Forgive me, my dear," Harry said with concern. "You appear peaked. Perhaps you'll feel better after you've eaten." He stood, waiving off the footman who came to his aid. "May I fix you a plate?"

Swallowing the lump in her throat, she replied, "Yes. Please. But not too much."

Moments later he placed a plate in front of her filled with coddled eggs, a thick slice of ham, and a biscuit with clotted cream and jam. Her mouth watered either from revolt or hunger. She would find out soon enough. "Thank you."

He made his way to his chair, sat, placed a napkin on his lap, and went back to eating. "If there's anything specific you would like for the morning meal, cook would be happy to prepare it. The same goes for midday and evening meals. Perhaps, when you feel more comfortable here, you will begin the duties expected of the lady of the house?"

Penelope's eyes lifted from the plate of food, which she'd yet to touch, except for the biscuit. Hoping to settle her insides and nerves, she nibbled on it. "I'd be happy to take over the duties from the housekeeper regarding the daily meals. I've not any experience in it, but how hard can it be?" She fervently hoped not hard at all.

"Splendid." He wiped his mouth with his napkin, stood, and bowed. "If you'll excuse me, I have things to attend to. I will see you at the evening meal."

Evening meal? Obviously, he had much to do on the day after their wedding. She needed to find something to occupy herself. She spent most of her life in service to the Viscount. Having idle time didn't arrive until she fled his house and became part of Wentworth's house as his half-sister. Leisurely time on her hands was something new to her, and she'd yet to be comfortable with it.

She made her way up the stairs to the family drawing room, thanks to directions from the young footman who blushed when she inquired of the room. She sat on a deep blue settee and rummaged through a basket filled with un-started needlepoint. Needlepoint was something she was quite adapt at, having learned from her mother, but never had much free time to accomplish anything but a small pillow. Same for embroidery. Inside the basket she found several white, clean handkerchiefs and decided she would embroider Harry's initials on them and present them as a late wedding gift.

Busy at work, she didn't realize the time flew by until a servant brought in the morning tea tray. At the same time the butler announced, "The Duchess of Wentworth, the Countess of Bridgeton, and the Countess of Northborough."

*Dear me, the day after the wedding and they all visit?* "Welcome. Please sit down. You have arrived at the correct time for tea." Penelope smiled to her family, sat down and poured tea for all. Strange how cook knew to expect visitors. "Did I not see all of you yesterday at my wedding?" Even she heard the sarcasm in her voice.

"Yes. Well," Bella, began, "we wanted to be assured you survived your wedding night."

Emma and Amelia both gasped out, "Bella!"

"Honestly," Bella huffed. "It's what you both are thinking. Our dear new sister marries a mysterious, scarred, one-eyed duke. A man rumored to work for the Crown in some secret capacity. Surely, we have a right to worry over her safety. Spies and gentlemen with dubious reputations could come and go in this house at all hours of the night and put our dear sister in danger."

Penelope laughed and nearly choked on her tea. "Really, Bella. What an imagination you have. I would expect it from Emma, our family gothic novelist, but you? Surely you don't really believe I'm in any danger from my husband or his associates?"

Bella looked at Emma and Amelia, silently pleading for help. Amelia took pity. "I believe our family history and the tragic events that seem to plague us has Bella worried." Amelia sipped her tea. "I'm not worried. The duke, although both handsome and scarred and mysterious all at the same time, appears to dote on you. Besides, Wentworth would never have married Penelope off to a degenerate."

Bella snorted most unladylike, "Well, let me remind you, Amelia, how our dear brother nearly married you off to a duke who was a degenerate of the first order. You barely escaped unscathed. The man tried to force himself on you."

Amelia's cheeks pinked and once again Penelope was hearing about the lives of her family members that she knew nothing about. So much had happened to them before she found them. Or rather, they found her after receiving her letter introducing herself. Penning that missive was one of the hardest things she'd ever done. Asking the family of her dead father for help, knowing she was a bastard and an embarrassment to them hadn't been easy. Somehow she'd mustered the courage and sent the letter off, praying someone in the Seabrook family would take pity on her and rescue her from her dire predicament. Now that she'd met the entire family she should not have worried. More kind, compassionate, and honorable people didn't exist. She tried to remind herself every day how lucky she was.

"Someday real soon, I wish to hear all the scandal, gossip, and stories that have followed our family and close friends, but not today. Today we're celebrating my marriage."

"Yes," Emma chimed in. "We came to hear about your wedding night."

Now it was Penelope's turn to blush. Surely they didn't expect her to share the intimate details of last night?

Of course, all the ladies present with her were married and had birthed children. So they... More heat suffused her cheeks at the thought of...

"You are blushing," Bella said. "Do we take that as a wonderful sign. That the marriage bed with the duke was... fulfilling for a better word."

All four of them giggled. "It was fine. He was kind and gentle."

Between nibbles on her biscuit, Emma said, "Good. Now let's talk about this monstrous house. It needs a feminine touch. Has His Grace said anything about making changes?"

"Actually, he has." Penelope looked around the drawing room. Although it was nice and cozy, it did need some updating and some brightening. Most all the rooms in the house were dreary. "I wouldn't even know where to begin."

"Say no more," Bella added. "I will help you. Since I recently remodeled Northborough Estate, I have the perfect designer and carpenters for you. Shall I send them over?"

For the second time, Penelope nearly choked on her tea.

"My goodness. I must discuss it with him. I don't think he expects me to remodel immediately. I need to get acclimated to being the lady of the house first."

"Sorry." Bella turned serious. "I've been distracted of late and was hoping for something to do. Selfish of me. Please forgive me."

Penelope had never seen Bella so somber and near tears before. Not that she'd known her all that long, but still. "When I do remodel, Bella, you will be the first person I contact for help. Meanwhile," she paused and studied Bella, "is there something amiss with you?"

After several moments, she finally wiped a stray tear from her eyes. "I lost a babe last week."

All three gasped. "Why didn't you say something." Amelia reached over and patted her sister on the knee.

"Because I had just confirmed it with the physician the week before. Hardly had time to get used to being with child and then..." She shook her head and wiped away her tears. "I'm fine. Myles took it hard. I know there will be more children, so that is what I'm looking ahead too. Also, I can't wait until our Penelope has news for us."

Third time she almost choked on her tea at the words coming out of her sister's mouths. "Yes. Well. I don't believe it happened last night. Doesn't it take time?"

Three sets of eyes looked amusingly at her. However, Emma was the first to speak. "Sometimes all it takes is one time. Perhaps you will be one of the fortunate brides to have conceived on your wedding night."

When she caught her breath from a coughing fit, she said, "Enough. Please. Someone tell me some juicy gossip?"

"Rumor has it Penelope Seabrook wed the Duke of Newbury in a hurried ceremony. Gossips speculate they were found in a compromising situation and her reputation would be in ruin if they didn't wed posthaste," Bella said with a hand flick and a laugh. "Honest. It was in the paper this morning. You asked for gossip."

Her stomach tightened. People were reading about her private life and gossiping about her and Newbury. And what they may or may not have done? Surely the privileged members of the ton had better things and people to gossip about. Her cheeks flamed. She hated people making speculations about her and Newbury. It was nobody's business but theirs.

It wasn't long after when her sisters and sister-in-law left and loneliness settled in. What would she do to occupy her time each day? She could only embroider so many handkerchiefs and needlepoint so many samplers and pillows. She'd never been one to nap in the afternoon. Perhaps she could take up watercolors. Silly, she'd never thought about painting before. She now had a life of leisure, she could do anything her heart desired.

Too bad the life of leisure didn't suit her. She needed a cause. Yes. That was it. Emma's cause of raising funds for the women and children in London. Too bad she hadn't thought of it when Emma was here earlier. She hurried upstairs to her chambers, sat down at her desk, and penned a note to Emma asking if she could help.

Perfect. She had a cause now. Since she'd lived the life of a servant, someone without means and money, someone who relied on the goodwill of a vile viscount, Penelope knew there were plenty of others out there who had been wronged. She intended to find them and offer up help.

Would the duke allow her to? Now that they were married, did she need to ask his permission? If the charity was run by Emma, he could hardly disapprove, could he?

# CHAPTER 9

"What do you mean he disappeared?" Harry bellowed to Edmond.

"Smythe never checked in last night."

Breathe. In and out. Keep breathing. If anything happened to Smythe, Harry would never forgive himself. He'd wanted the Runner working for him. Working with him. Because of him, he was missing. Tension coiled inside every muscle and tendon in his body. "Bloody hell. Put Franklin and Broderick on it. Meanwhile, I'll go out and see what I can find. Hopefully he's fine, just in too deep to pull out and make check-in. When was his last known contact?"

"Night before last. With Franklin just outside the Hounds of Hell Pub in St. Giles."

"I'll start there," Harry said as tingles of awareness traveled up his spine. If he was a betting man he'd bet Smythe was at the pub. Only question was, was he there of his own accord? Or was his cover blown, and he was being held prisoner. Only one way to find out. This called for Harry's disguise that very few members of the War Office knew about. Desperate times called for desperate measure.

However, there was something he had to take care of before he left. He found Penelope in the family drawing room making a list. This was not how he planned on telling her about his dual identity only a sennight into their marriage. But God forbid something should happen to him while out looking for Smythe and he never returned. He needed to clear the air with Penelope. It would be shocking enough if she learned of his death but to learn of his deceit would be unthinkable.

Harry entered the drawing room and closed the door so they wouldn't be disturbed. "I was hoping to speak with you before I leave for the War Office."

She stopped writing, placed her lap desk on the coffee table and said, "Please sit and tell me what has you so unsettled."

How could she tell? He forwent his cane, leaving it by the closed door. He never put his knee brace on that morning, so he walked quite normally to a chair opposite the settee she resided on. And decided not to mince words but get right to the point of what he had to say. He only hoped she forgave him eventually for his deceit.

With her inquisitive blue eyes on his face, he slid off his patch and removed his make-up with his handkerchief. The only sound he heard was her gasp. Her hand flew to her mouth, and her eyes widened with disbelief. After that, nothing. Uncomfortable silence hovered around the room. Soon her eyes narrowed into stormy slits, her cheeks reddened, and he waited for her temper to explode.

When still she said nothing he couldn't stand the silence any longer. "I'm sorry. I've been trying to tell you since we wed. Truthfully, since we met, but how to explain that Harry and Hugh are the same person?" The sound of her inhaling and exhaling had him pausing, believing she wanted to speak. When she didn't, he continued. "I work for the War

Office as a spy. To do my job, I have different identities. I'm Harry. Although most people think I'm a cripple, I'm perfectly normal as you can see. I created Hugh and the injured Harry so I could move within society without anyone truly knowing what capacity Hugh or Harry had inside the War Office. I also have two more identities I use when I go deep undercover." He paused, stood, and began pacing back and forth across the room.

"Which is why I needed to explain all this before I leave today." He paused in front of her and swallowed down the guilt eating him alive at the look of hurt, pain, and shock marring her beautiful face.

"First you need to know that I never enjoyed deceiving you. I hated having to. And I know it's too much to ask of you now, but I hope in the near future you'll find it in your heart to forgive me." He scrubbed his hands down his face, hoping for words of wisdom. None came. "I don't blame you if you hate me."

"I don't."

His eyes locked with hers. "You don't?"

"No. I feel many things, but shockingly, hate isn't one of them." She paused and ran her hands down her skirt. "Some part of me is relieved. Another part of me wants to hurl everything I can get my hands on in this room at you because I'm so angry. But most of all, I'm hurt. Beyond hurt. When I have time to think and go back to the very beginning, not when I met you at the Spencers' for a dinner party but when you were being Hugh. How I made a fool of myself, I'm sure even more anger will come crashing over me." She stopped running her hands up and down her skirt and clutched the fabric tight and twisted. "I want to scream. I want to run and hide. But mostly I want to hit you."

"Good. Get your anger out. I don't blame you. But know that I had no choice in the beginning but to deceive you. The life of the people I work with and my own relied on my deceit. After we wed, I'll admit I've been trying to tell you the truth. But I failed you. I'm sorry. Be angry with me, but remember there were many lives I needed to protect. And know that we are one now, and I must protect your life." He began pacing again. "I'm going deep undercover, looking for one of my men. I needed you to know the truth before I leave." He stopped in front of her and bowed. "I bid you good day, my dear."

THAT WAS IT. "I bid you good day, my dear" and he left without another word. Before she could yell and scream and throw things at him? Not that she would actually throw objects at him, and she'd had her chance to yell at him and she chose not to. Chose not to because he looked as though his best friend had died. Behind his apology and explanation was filled with deep regret and sorrow. How could she yell at him when he truly felt sorry for deceiving her? Oh, she knew later that day when she processed all that transpired between them since the very first meeting, she would be beyond angry. But right now she was in too much shock to feel much of anything, except the look in his eyes as he bowed to her, plagued her mind. It appeared as though he was saying good-bye. That they would never see each other again. She jumped up and hurried down the hallway to his chambers and knocked on the door. Edmond, his valet, opened it and bowed.

"May I help you, Your Grace?"

"I need to see Har...His Grace."

"He left."

Without another word, she swallowed the lump forming in her throat. Fear gripped her heart, and she walked to her room, shut the door behind her, and fell onto her bed on her back. Staring up at the plastered ceiling, and prayed the ominous feeling that spread inside her body quicker than a kitchen fire wasn't a sign of what would come. She prayed Harry would be safe. That she would see him again. Be able to explain that she understood why he did what he did. Even if truthfully, she didn't. But she did. Confusion and worry for Harry's safety overwhelmed her until her eyes closed and she fell asleep.

HARRY HATED LEAVING Penelope the way he had. But he had no choice. He'd brought Smythe into the inner circle of his spies, and he was responsible for his safety. He'd already lost two members of his team, he refused to lose another. He left by the servants' stairs, dressed in shabby dockworker clothes, and hailed a hackney to take him to the Hounds of Hell Pub where Smythe was last seen.

A Mr. Fitzpatrick who ran the underbelly of St. Giles owned and operated the pub. He was the man sane persons feared most. Anyone who went against him was usually found floating in the Thames, bloated and nibbled on by fish. Harry shivered beneath his tattered coat. Not because of the chill in the air, but because icy talons of death crawled up his spine, warning him. He would bring Smythe home, dead or alive. He owed it to the man and his wife. And Penelope? He owed her everything. All that he was and would be. Would he live to tell her? Beg her forgiveness and tell her he loved her? Only time would tell. Time he didn't have if he hoped to save Smythe. If it wasn't too late already.

As two drunks stumbled out the doors of the pub, Harry slithered in hopefully unnoticed. He took a seat facing the door at a table in a dark corner where he had a view of most of the pub. Middle of the afternoon, the place was quiet. In another hour or two the dock workers would come in by the droves looking to quench their thirst and fill their bellies. A young serving wench with greasy brown hair, tired and bruised features, and a stained dress showing off her generous bosom approached his table with a wary smile. Someone had smacked her around recently. That someone deserved to be beaten.

"What canna get ya?"

"Pitcher of ale and some bread."

"Com'n right up."

The ale was barely drinkable, the bread was something else entirely. He pushed it aside and sipped on his watery mug of ale, biding his time. Watching and listening. His hat pulled low on his head, hiding his eyes from view. Every time the door opened, the serving wench started and her eyes flew to the person or persons entering. Once she got a good look at the person or persons stepping over the threshold she relaxed. It wasn't until Fitzpatrick came in through the kitchen that Harry saw her turn white and shrink into herself. So the big man himself caused her bruises. And what brought him to this pub in particular? He owned dozens around the city. Did it have anything to do with Smythe? Most likely it did. Harry would reserve one room on the second or third floor for the night and hope Smythe was being held in another. *Please don't let him be dead and fish food in the Thames.*

Next time he saw the wench, he passed her a coin. "I need a room for the night." She disappeared, only to come back moments later with a key. "Room 205. 'Nother shilling if ya wan clean linens and towels." He gave her two. "Be back when tis ready."

By the time his room was ready the pub was crawling with dock workers, the stench of fish, ale, and whatever came from the kitchens. Christ, he'd be forced to order the barely edible food for himself soon before the ale went to his head. When the tired wench came back, he gave her more coin. "Please, some decent food."

Not long after, she came back with a bowl of stew that smelled and looked quite good and bread that wasn't crawling with mealy worms. And a crock of clotted cream that looked fairly fresh. Coin talked. Perhaps if he offered her enough and his protection, she would tell him about Fitzpatrick or Littleton.

Several boring hours went by. Harry noticed Edmond come in and sit down with some slimy workers and join their hand of cards. He hoped he knew what he was doing. They looked like a dangerous bunch. But then again, so didn't everyone in the place. Not that Edmond couldn't handle dangerous. He could. Which was why Harry relied on him most in perilous situations such as this.

# CHAPTER 10

PENELOPE SAT IN THE FAMILY DRAWING ROOM, THE ONLY LIGHT coming from the blazing hearth and the one candle she'd brought with her. Since it was the middle of the night, the room had been chilled when she arrived. Her long ago skill in building a fire served her well as she ignited a warm orange flame in the hearth. Dragging a chair close to the fire, she sat down with a deep, wary sigh. Her body ached, as well as her heart, making her feel years older. Ever since Harry left that afternoon, there'd been no word from him. Even his valet had disappeared. No one in the house seemed to know where he went or when he would return.

Now that she knew about his dangerous job, his actual job, anxiety had her unable to sleep for worry about his safety. Surely, no good would come of being gone at all hours of the night.

Her mind still grappled with trying to make sense of what he explained about his life. How he had multiple personas. One good thing came of his explanation, though, she no longer felt guilty about being attracted to both Harry and Hugh. It made perfect sense that she would be attracted to

Hugh, as he was Harry. One small consolation from the awkward and enlightening conversation.

A slight noise behind her had her heart accelerating in anticipation that Harry had come home to her. "Welcome home, Harry."

No answer. Before she could turn around and wonder if she'd imagined the quiet footsteps, a middle-aged man dressed in black stood before her. "Sorry to disappoint you, Your Grace, but your husband is not home. It is I, Baron Littleton." He toyed with a small brown glass bottle in his hand. "Will you come with me willingly and quietly, or will I need to drug you?"

Go with him? Was he out of his mind? Who was this man, and why would he want her with him? Her eyes widened and her heart slammed against her chest as reality dawned on her. This was Harry's enemy. Her mind screamed out to go peacefully with him. That all would be well if she didn't resist. Her body had other ideas. Either she tried to escape and scream for help, or she fought him with her person. Either way, she would lose. Too bad she didn't listen to her mind telling her to be reasonable.

She flew to her feet, brought up both hands, and shoved the man back. He stumbled for a moment since she'd caught him off guard. She turned to flee, inhaling a deep breath, ready to scream for help. A hand reached out, grabbed her elbow, swung her around. He grabbed her lips, forcing her mouth open, and poured a vile tasting liquid into her mouth. Laudanum. Before she could spit it out, he clamped her jaw closed, and she had no choice but to swallow. Dizziness surrounded her as she felt her legs give way and blackness descend all around her.

~

"WELL, well, well, you have finally awakened." The man's voice from the drawing room penetrated through her foggy mind. She tried to speak, but her mouth appeared sealed shut. So dry. The taste awful. For several moments she licked her lips, trying to moisten them and her mouth so she could form words.

"Where am I?" Her voice came out low and deep.

"You are safe…for now."

Her eyes moved around the room, taking in her surroundings. Behind the brown velvet curtains lightness peeked around the window. Morning had come. Or afternoon. She had no way of knowing how long she'd been out from the vile drug. The moment it had hit her tongue, she'd known it was laudanum. The way he recklessly poured it into her mouth, it was a wonder she woke up at all. "Where am it?" she repeated.

Deep laughter traveled to her ears. "You are safe…for now. If you try to escape or scream for help, neither of which will aid you, I'll be forced to tie you up and keep you drugged. The choice is yours, my dear. Easy or hard. Either way, I don't care. I'm only using you to get to your dreadful husband."

Her heart sank. He was using her. Why else had he taken her. Did Harry care enough about her to get her back? Rescue her? See her safely back home? Perhaps not. No. No. She must not think that way. He would find her. She had to believe that. If he didn't care for her, he never would have married her. Which he did willingly. She needed to believe in him in order to survive her captivity. "I'll not try to escape or call out. You have my word."

"Your word," he spat out with a snort. "The word of a bastard. A tragic day in society when a bastard becomes a duchess. Even worse, when Harry became a duke. The prince really needs to be more careful with whom he surrounds himself. Now, if you'll excuse me, I have a duke to reason with."

The click of the lock turning in the door had her realizing she truly was a prisoner. Looking around her, she found herself in a small, stuffy, dreary room with only a small bed and dresser and the chair she sat on. Most likely servants' quarters. Was the baron daft enough to have brought her to his London residence? Perhaps. Perhaps not. Did it really matter? No. A prisoner was a prisoner no matter where she was held captive.

She stood on wobbly legs and paced the small room, feeling closed in, and finding it hard to breathe. On the dresser sat a tray. She inspected it and found barely warm tea, a hard cold roll, and eggs. With her stomach unsettled, she sipped the tea and nibbled the hard roll as she continued her pacing. When she finally sank down into the wooden chair, she heard footsteps coming from the room beside hers. Was there someone else being held captive?

She tiptoed in her slippers to the wall. Why she tiptoed she did not know. She pressed her ear against the wall and listened to the footsteps. The turning of a key. The creaking of a door. Then the unmistakable voice of the baron. Only he spoke quietly. She could not make out what he was saying. Once in a while she recognized a word, but not enough to understand what he said. Or whom he said it to.

After he left, she raised her hand to the wall and knocked and spoke. "Hello. Is someone there?"

A knock back. Then a man's voice. "Yes. Smythe here. Who are you?"

"Penelope. Duchess of Newbury."

"My God. How did you?" Silence. "Never mind. Harry will come for you. And that is the problem. He wants him dead. The French want him dead. Actually, more than dead, they want information. They will hold you hostage until they have what they need, then torture and murder him."

Penelope gasped, one hand covering her mouth, the other her heart. Harry dead? The thought paralyzed her insides. "He mustn't come here." If anything happened to him, how would she forgive herself. If he hadn't married her, none of this would be happening. Her heart believed that, but her mind knew otherwise. If the French wanted information and death for Harry, they would have found another way. If not through her, through someone or something else.

"He will come. You're his wife. His responsibility. From what I've gathered in the little time I've worked with him, no more honorable man exists elsewhere. The people he worked for and with say it, so it is so. He will come. To him he will have no choice. His honor won't let him do otherwise."

That was what she was afraid of. He would be honor bound to save her. He could send his people, but he wouldn't. He alone would be obligated to come for her. Tears stung the back of her eyes when she thought of never seeing him again. Never kissing him. Holding him. Seeing his handsome face, with or without his disguise, across the dining table. Never waltzing with him. Or making love. Or carrying his babe. No longer were the tears burning her eyes, they were running freely down her cheeks. She didn't bother wiping them away as more would only take their place. Instead of continuing her conversation with Smythe, she crawled on the small bed, curled into a ball, cried, and prayed Harry stayed away from her. From this vile place that would only bring forth his death.

# CHAPTER 11

"It's about time you returned."

Harry's head snapped up at the sound of the dreaded voice of his enemy, Baron Littleton, in his home.

"Nothing to say? Tis a pity as your lovely duchess had much to say when I intruded in her private space."

Harry's heart stopped. Penelope. The bastard spoke with Penelope. Or worse? "Where is she?" he demanded as his heart started up again three times the normal beat.

"She's unharmed. For the time being. It all depends on your cooperation."

"If you harm one hair on her head..."

"Tsk, tsk, tsk. Threatening me will not help her cause."

Harry fought down the urge to wrap his hands around Littleton's neck. "I ask again, where is my wife?"

"As I said, she's unharmed. But you should've kept her safer. Entering your home was easy then and now." The baron grinned, but his eyes glared with hatred. "Shall we sit and converse like the civilized gentlemen we are? By the way, you have excellent whiskey. Goes down smooth as silk. I helped myself."

Harry's blood boiled. Civilized. The intruder was as far from civilized as one could be. He swallowed his pride and anger, intent on only getting answers about Penelope. He gestured toward the two chairs facing the hearth in his sitting room. "Please have a seat. Would you like me to send for a tray?" Christ, he didn't just offer the man food, did he? Surely his mind was not working properly. He should arrest the bastard and be done with him.

The baron smirked. "Thank you. But no. I've eaten. More of that fine whiskey would be nice though."

Biting back a growl, Harry made his way to the sideboard and poured generous amounts of whiskey into two crystal tumblers and handed one off to Littleton. He sat and sipped his, all the time eyeing the baron. Most of his people would squirm at being scrutinized by him, but not this man. He had the heart and soul of granite. How else could one explain the heinous crimes the man committed against his own countrymen.

"You must tell me who your supplier is. I must get my hands on this whiskey," Baron Littleton said as he sipped the liquid.

"I'm afraid I don't know. It was a gift." Harry inhaled and tried to make sense of the words scrambling inside his head, trying to come out all at once. "You didn't come here to discuss whiskey. Tell me what you want and where my wife is? I could arrest you right now and throw your arse in jail."

"Come now, Newbury, I'm holding all the best cards here. No need to be rude. If you arrest me, you will never get your wife or Smythe back. That's right, I have him as well. As for what I want, I want my name cleared. My title and holdings restored to me. When that happens I will gladly return your wife to you unharmed. And as a bonus I'll give you Smythe too." He paused, drained his glass, and stood. "Until then I will keep your lovely wife." The bastard bowed. "I have two men posted outside. Send word to them when you are ready to negotiate. I hope your relationship with Prinny is good. All this rests in his hands."

Once alone, Harry's arm came up, and he flung his glass into the fire. The sound of crystal hitting brick and flames made quite a loud crashing sound. Unfortunately, Harry experienced no satisfaction from his show of anger. Anger, frustration, and worry for Penelope. He paced the room, hands combing through his hair. His heart beat wildly against his chest as he tried to think. "Think, damn you, think," he yelled to himself. When nothing came to him, he changed into his Duke of Newbury persona. Unable to find Edmond, he made his way to the foyer and ordered his carriage brought around from the mews. He didn't care if it was the middle of the night. He had to see Prinny. Had to beg for his wife's safety.

Whatever it took, he would see the baron's title and lands restored to him. Once done and Penelope was back safe and sound, he would take the bastard down. Littleton would pay for his crimes—past and present.

AFTER MEETING WITH PRINNY, Harry had in his possession the deeds and title Littleton had been stripped of. Even though both he and Prinny knew it was a trap to capture Harry, they decided to go along with the baron for now. Give him what he asked for and the Prince Regent would take it back at a later time. The most important thing was to get Penelope back. And Smythe. At least Penelope wasn't alone. Or was she? Were they being kept at different locations? Even if the location was the same, they no doubt were in separate rooms, cells, or dungeons. Harry had no way of knowing.

As for Penelope's safety, he had to take the baron's word she was safe. But safe could mean anything from being kept in a dark, damp cell with food and water to a comfortable room. So as not to drive his mind crazy, he pictured her in comfort. Surely Littleton would treat a lady properly.

Harry penned a missive for Littleton and sent it off to his London residence. The only residence not entailed to the title. Therefore, it remained in Littleton's ownership. Could he be daft enough to be holding Penelope there? Harry would find out soon enough. Regardless of what Littleton said in his return correspondence, Harry and his men would invade his London residence this very night, hoping to rescue his wife and Smythe. If all failed, then Harry would dangle the baron's estates and title before him.

Harry was prepared to give himself up as additional payment if the plans tonight didn't work first. He'd met with his barrister earlier to have the necessary papers drawn up to ensure Penelope was taken care of. As Harry had no relatives he knew of, the title and all entailed properties would go back to the crown. Unless...his wife carried his babe. A male heir. Harry rubbed his aching chest. Would he live to see the day Penelope gave birth to his heir? Or even live to have a daughter. A precious girl who looked very much like her mother? Harry, never one to be sentimental, found himself being just that.

"Enough," he yelled, "enough." He needed to be strong, hard, and fearless. It was the only way he would rescue her and keep himself alive.

Late that evening he headed to Littleton's London residence. Everything tonight hinged on his hunch that Littleton held Penelope and Smythe at his London residence. His driver dropped him off several houses down, and Newbury made his way in his Newbury disguise. Edmond and five of his best men surrounded the place. Fifteen minutes after he entered the townhome, they were to take out Littleton's men patrolling the exterior then enter cautiously, knowing more armed men would be inside. Once they were neutralized, Littleton would be taken into custody—Penelope and Smythe released. Harry prayed all went well. From past experiences he knew there were always glitches. Not this time, please. Not this time. He'd never had anything personal at stake before. How brilliant of Littleton to use his new wife to accomplish what he wanted. Harry would remember that tactic in the future. And guard Penelope much more carefully. How neglectful he was in failing her even once.

A young, strong butler answered the door and let him in. No butler at all, but a French spy. Harry had an extra sense when it came to spies. Hence, why he was so good at his profession. Why Prinny worked hard to keep him on. Truth-be-told, after tonight, he may hang up his spy hat and retire so he could enjoy his wife. Spend time in the country and perhaps go on an extended honeymoon on the continent.

"This way, Your Grace."

Harry followed the butler up the grand staircase, down a hallway, and into Littleton's office, he presumed.

"Welcome, Newbury." Littleton gestured toward a brown leather chair that faced a large mahogany desk. "Please sit." He held up a crystal decanter filled halfway with amber liquid. "A drink of brandy before we get down to the business at hand?"

"Please," Harry replied, trying to remain calm and not lunge across the desk and ring the man's neck and demand to see his wife.

Once settled, each with a glass in hand, Littleton raised his brows in silent question.

Harry scoffed. "I met with Prinny." He reached into his

inner coat pocket and threw a large envelope onto the desk top. "Everything you asked for returned to you." Harry waited until the baron scoured the documentation before he continued. "Now. I would like to collect my wife and leave without further ado."

"Yes. Yes. One moment please."

Chills of warning crawled up Harry's spine and he knew Littleton stalled for time. Perhaps he didn't have it in him to kill him and instead waited upon the butler's return to do the deed. Too bad killing him wouldn't be all that easy. Because Harry could hear the commotion coming from down the hall. His men had arrived. Harry whipped out his pistol, cocked it, and aimed it at Littleton's head. "I wouldn't move if I were you. I have a twitchy finger. One never knows when it will…twitch."

Littleton's face drained of blood. "Come now, Newbury. We had a deal. I get what I want and you get your wife. You didn't even give me time to have my butler retrieve her from her room. A room I might add that had all the comforts of home.

Penelope heard voices and banging from downstairs. Hurried footsteps rushing by her door. Her pulse roared. Something was happening. Could she dare get her hopes up? Had Harry stormed the front door, knocking aside all who got in his way to rescue her? Her mind resembled one of Emma's gothic novels. When her door did not crash open, she tried to hide her disappointment as noises came from Smythe's room next door.

"It's about bloody time you arrived." Smythe's voice was recognizable through the wall.

"You're bloody shit lucky we came for your sorry arse at

all." A voice she thought was Harry's valet, Edmond. Was he in the organization as well? Before she had her answer, the man she'd come to know as Littleton and Harry bolted through her door. Just as her husband reached her, the baron somehow shoved him aside. He then wrapped a hard arm around her waist. His other hand raised a blade to her neck.

"You better not move if you want to see tomorrow," Littleton said, breathing hard as though he'd run up the stairs and down the hall, which he no doubt had.

She screamed, "Harry!"

He looked more like Hugh than Harry since his cane was gone, his patch missing. The only resemblance to Harry was the fake scar.

"Don't move," Harry barked. "Please don't move."

She froze, afraid to move, frightened the baron would kill her anyway as a means to punish Harry. He hated Harry and all the good he stood for. The baron and the people he worked with, and for, had no moral compass. He wouldn't think twice littering the ground with dead bodies. Oh, dear. She gasped. Stop thinking terrible thoughts. Think positive. Harry won't let anything happen to her. But what about him?

"What do you want now, Littleton?" Harry asked, standing feet apart, arms across his chest, looking for all the world as though nothing were amiss.

"What I was promised. Freedom to take my title and lands and live my life in safety. I'll give up my spying for France and your lovely wife."

"How do I know you will hold up your end of the bargain? That you will not continue to spy for France? That you won't exact revenge on those who have wronged you?" Harry said with an even tone.

To Penelope's way of thinking, he gave nothing away. Showed no emotion. Meanwhile, her insides tumbled over and over again. Her pulse pounded inside her ears, and she thought she might faint from lack of air. She'd never fainted in her entire life and would not let it happen now. Think, think, she said to herself. What could she do to distract the baron?

Littleton laughed. "You don't. You just have to trust me."

Before Harry could answer, several things happened at once. A crowd of men entered her room with guns in their hands pointed at Littleton. The baron, momentarily distracted, loosened his grip on her waist and at her throat. Harry crashed forward, smacked the knife from the man's hand, and Harry fell to the floor with her. He twisted so his body took the brunt of the force. She landed hard on him, the air knocked from her lungs, and it took her time to be able to breathe normally. By then, two of the other men marched Littleton by gunpoint out of the room. No doubt he would hang for his crimes to the crown. Penelope tried to feel bad for him, but according to her husband he'd caused many innocent lives to be lost and she could not find it in her.

Once most everyone was gone, Harry helped her stand and hugged her close. His body trembled as hard as hers, and she wrapped her arms around his waist and held on as tears of relief streamed down her cheeks.

"Before I leave," the one man still in the room said, who looked an awful lot like Mary Spencer's husband, "is there anything you need, Your Grace?"

"No, Smythe. With Littleton in custody, I'm taking my wife home and begging her forgiveness. I suggest you do the same with yours."

Smythe bowed. "Thank you." He nodded his head, acknowledging Penelope. "I hope to see you under better circumstances next time we meet."

"Yes," was all she could manage as he exited the room. As

Harry led her toward the door and freedom she said, "Was that Mary Spencer's new husband?"

"Yes indeed."

Her head snapped his way just as they entered their carriage. "Does everyone you associate with work for the Crown?"

"Not everyone."

# CHAPTER 12

WHEN HARRY AND LITTLETON CRASHED THROUGH THE DOOR and Littleton beat him to Penelope, Harry nearly fell to his knees in panic. Instead, he took up a relaxed stance and used words to stall for time. He knew reinforcements would come soon. He just had to stall the baron long enough for them to arrive. Keep him talking. Make him believe he still had a chance to get out of there without being taken into custody. Stupid man.

When his men came into the room it was the perfect time to make his move. Littleton had relaxed his guard for a moment, and Newbury took advantage by charging him, using his hand to knock the knife from Littleton and bring Penelope down to the ground safely. Ever since that frightening incident, she'd been unfocused, too distracted to notice he'd wrapped the new handkerchief she embroidered for him around his hand, which had been sliced good and deep from the blade. Even now the blood seeped through the fine linen cloth.

"What happened?" she said with a frown as she reached

for his arm. He kept it out of reach. She didn't need his blood all over her.

"Cut by Littleton's knife. I'll have Edmond stitch it up and I'll be good as new in no time."

Silence. Why was she staring at his hand and saying not a word?"

Finally, after several torturous moments, she spoke very softly. "Do you do this sort of dangerous work all the time?"

How to answer the question truthfully? "Sometimes. Not always. Most of my time is spent watching and waiting. Confrontations like this happen rarely." Well, rarely did they involve one's wife. He hadn't actually lied. "Let's go home and when you're rested, we can talk."

TALK. Penelope wasn't sure she ever wanted to talk about what happened. Or rather, what could have happened if things hadn't gone their way. A chill creeped up her spine as she sat in the sitting room that connected her bedchamber to Harry's. She pulled tight on her dressing robe, hoping it would help alleviate the chill. Unfortunately, the flames from the hearth did little to warm her. Perhaps because it was the middle of the night, and she hadn't slept in some time, which added to her chill. Being drugged with laudanum and unconscious didn't count as sleeping.

What was taking her husband so long? He said he would meet with her here after he freshened up. That was hours ago, and she wanted to see him and be reassured his injury was minor. That he wasn't hiding something from her. It didn't bode well for their marriage if she believed he was hiding truths from her. Ever since Hadley's employ, trust didn't come easy to her.

The creak of a door and soft footsteps had her head

turning toward her husband. He looked relaxed in his shirt-sleeves rolled up to his elbows, trousers, and bare feet. Recently bathed, if his damp hair was any sign. His hand was newly bandaged with clean linen.

"Hello, my dear," he said as he strolled toward her and took a seat on the settee beside her. "You look well. How do you feel?"

His concern for her warmed her heart, which helped expel the chill from her body. "I'm fine, now that I'm safe at home." She gently reached for his injured arm. "How is your hand? Did you need stitches?"

"It's fine and yes. Edmond does superb work."

Tension was a living, breathing thing between them. Penelope wondered when it would vanish and be replaced with relaxation for good. Being tense all the time wasn't good for either of them. It was no way to live within a marriage. She would take the first steps now in helping their marriage along. "I understand why you deceived me in being both Harry and Hugh. Today was eye-opening into the life you lead."

"Please don't think it's always like this." He wrapped his arm around her waist and pulled her close. She snuggled against him, feeling calm spread throughout her body for the first time since they arrived home. "Thank God it's not usually like tonight. And I promise you, I will let no one kidnap you or use you to get to me ever again. I will never let my guard down. You will be safe. I promise."

Penelope knew it would take time for the events of the day to fade into her memory. Meanwhile she would trust her husband to keep her safe.

Harry made love to her on the settee in front of the warm hearth before he took her hand and led her to her bed where he spent the night holding her tight as she slept.

## CHAPTER 13

A WEEK LATER WENTWORTH WAS HOSTING A DINNER PARTY with all their friends in honor of Penelope and Harry.

Her stomach had butterflies visiting her. A week had gone by since her abduction and subsequent rescue. She'd not seen her family since. Harry had wanted her all to himself. According to him, he had much to atone for. They spent the past week with him atoning.

Their lovemaking reached levels Penelope never knew existed. People only talked about a woman's duty to her husband when it came to the marital bed. Strange no one admitted how beautiful, satisfying, and utterly emotionally connected two souls could become. She could hardly remember a time without him. He'd become her everything.

As she thought of her husband, he appeared in her bedchamber just as her maid put the finishing touches to her hair. Beautiful butterfly sapphire and diamond hair clips. A generous gift from Harry. He purchased them new, not liking most of the Sinclair family jewels.

"That will be all, Clarisse," Penelope said with a smile when she caught Harry's eyes in the mirror. Dark blue eyes that never failed to move her. To the outside world it would appear as though Hugh Sinclair escorted her to her family home this evening. Harry still had to go around town in his disguise. As he told her earlier in the day, to the whole of the ton he was a cripple and would have to stay a cripple at least until he resigned from the War Office.

Rising from her chair, she spun in a circle, sending her royal blue skirts swishing around her legs. "How do I look?"

Her husband's eyes darkened, and his smile faltered. "Too good to take you to your brother's for dinner." He stepped closer to her. Except it was more like a prowl. He took her lips in a deep probing kiss that curled her toes inside her silk slippers.

"You look good enough to eat." His deeper than normal voice said, "And I'm famished."

Penelope laughed and stepped out of his reach. "We mustn't be late. You know how Thomas can be."

Harry expelled a laugh. "Yes. Let us be on our way then."

As it turned out they were the last to arrive, and all eyes turned toward them as the butler announced their arrival.

"Everyone is staring at us," Penelope whispered.

Harry patted her hand. "Not us, dear. They are looking at you as you look divine."

She laughed and shook her head. "You are so wrong. It's the first time you have ventured out in public without your Duke of Newbury disguise. They don't know what to make of you. Which I may add, is very kind and trusting of you to trust my family to keep your secret.

Wentworth and Bella hurried over. "Newbury, Penelope, welcome," said her brother. After bows and greetings, Wentworth said, "Nice to see you as yourself, Newbury. No more disguise."

Bella's eyes widened. "You knew and didn't enlighten me?"

Wentworth shrugged a shoulder. "Come, let us make the rounds."

Penelope's sisters were there with their husbands. The Earl of Northborough and the Earl of Bridgeton. Also in attendance was the Marquess and Marchioness of Amesbury. Mr. Stuart Spencer and his lovely wife, Miranda, and Mr. Smythe and his wife, Mary. It shocked Penelope when she saw her other brother, Sebastian and his wife, Teagan. All her family and friends, except for the Dowager Duchess, were in attendance.

Standing in the drawing room, on the arm of her husband, there wasn't anywhere else in the world she'd rather be. She'd been blessed with more than she deserved since her humble beginnings. And never would she take anything or anyone for granted.

# EPILOGUE

"Mama, Papa, look at me." A chubby, blond, blue-eyed boy of three was riding his pony with the help of a groomsman. "I ride good."

"Yes, you do, Henry," both parents said at once then they laughed.

Seven years and four children had Penelope and Harry either finishing each other's sentences or speaking simultaneously.

They were blissfully happy with three daughters, Prudence, Catherine, Hillary and Henry, the heir.

"Sweetheart." Penelope glowed, her hand going to her stomach. "Do you think we have room for one more?"

"Yes," Harry bellowed, as he swept her up in his arms, and gently swung her around. "Yes, yes, a million yeses. I love you."

Her heart pitter-patted hearing those words come from her fearless spy of a husband. "I love you."

That night as their children slept, Harry and Penelope showered each other with their love.

The End

# ABOUT THE AUTHOR

Christine Donovan is an International Bestselling Author who writes romance that touches the heart, soothes the soul and feeds the mind. She is a PAN Member of RWA and belongs to Novelist, Inc. and Rhode Island Romance Writers. She lives on the Southeast Coast of Massachusetts with her husband. She has four grown sons, one granddaughter and three cats. As well as writing historical romance set in the regency era, she also writes contemporary and paranormal. In her spare time, she can be found at the beach, reading, painting or gardening. She loves to tackle DIY projects. Please visit her at http://www.authorchristinedonovan.com

www.ingramcontent.com/pod-product-compliance
Lightning Source LLC
Chambersburg PA
CBHW051944170626
46808CB00007B/2469